Echoes *of* My Son

A Novel

EUGENE H. STRAYHORN JR.

ISBN 978-1-964097-89-3 (hardcover)
ISBN 978-1-964097-69-5 (softcover)
ISBN 978-1-964097-70-1 (ebook)

This book is a work of fiction. Names, characters, places, and incidents are the product of the author's imagination or are used fictitiously. Any resemblance to actual locales, events, or persons, living or dead, is purely coincidental.

Printed in the United States of America.

INK START MEDIA
265 Eastchester Dr Ste 133 #102
High Point NC 27262

CONTENTS

1

LOSS BEYOND MEASURE

March 21, 2017

What one thing does a person cherish most dearly? What is to be valued above all else?

Some might claim it's our ability to draw breath. Others would say it's having enough food to eat or adequate shelter. Yet though necessary, these gifts are often taken for granted, as are many of life's blessings. Sadly, there are some who never pause long enough to puzzle out what they prize most until it is too late. They learn the worth of a thing only after it has been taken away.

This is precisely what happened to Reid Scott.

On a blustery March day, Reid stood gazing out through the front windows of ERA Inc., his privately owned software development firm. As the sole owner and CEO, he insisted on knowing everything that went on in his company. Even the smallest problems were to be brought to his attention.

Experience had taught him that what you don't know will someday hurt you. Yet supervising daily operations was not the reason he was running late.

His revolutionary new software product was ready to be introduced to the transportation industry, and for six hours, he had been in final negotiations with the company that could make it happen.

Hammering out a viable contract had demanded patience and great skill. The process had proven tedious and, at times, contentious. Yet twenty minutes earlier, all relevant documents had been signed by both parties. The deal would stand as a milestone in ERA's evolution.

His company's financial solvency was now guaranteed for the next eighteen months. Beyond that—well, that was a concern for another day.

A tracery of clouds the color of burnished gold dotted the twilight sky as Reid exited ERA's main entrance.

That afternoon, Allison, his wife of twenty-one years, had called to inform him that dinner was to be a special occasion—a celebration of some very good news. He had refrained from seeking details; all would be revealed eventually. Allison enjoyed her little surprises.

Reid checked his watch. Having promised to be home by five thirty, he was going to be seriously late. Even so, he smiled with satisfaction as he recalled how deftly he had overcome one sticking point after another.

This night, the Scotts would have two reasons to celebrate. He stepped off the curb and strode across the parking lot.

After graduating from Stanford with a bachelor's degree in computer science, Reid had elected to skip graduate school. Instead, he had launched his career as a software developer. In those early days, the computer industry in Silicon Valley was one of the most competitive environments imaginable.

Hard work and personal discipline had paid off. Reid's subsequent successes had proven nothing short of phenomenal. The result was that, at forty-six, his net worth had soared to heights most people could only dream about.

Reid pressed the Lexus RC turbo's starter button. Its powerful engine roared to life. With ease, he navigated surface streets that wound through the outskirts of Mountain View, California. Making good time, he accelerated onto the main thoroughfare that would take him home to Menlo Park and the surprise that awaited him.

Allison Scott watched the second hand slowly sweep the gilded face of the clock on the marble-top sideboard. When it pointed straight up, she heaved a sigh heavy with frustration.

Her husband was exactly two hours late. Dinner had long since grown cold. The meal could be reheated, of course, but that wasn't the issue. What distressed her most was that she had lost her happy frame of mind. Glad tidings, like cheap wine, tended to sour when bottled up too long.

Seated alone at the long dining room table, Allison had defaulted to her customary station: the chair nearest the kitchen. Her eyes swept the room. The honey-walnut dinner table gleamed with a muted luster. The family's Wedgwood dinner service filled the china buffet, the plates and saucers arranged in orderly rows. Three of the twelve place settings had been carefully placed on the table.

A blue-gray Persian rug covered most of the room's hardwood flooring. Its hand-knotted floral pattern screamed expensive elegance, as did the gold leaf mirror above the sideboard. Such were the trappings of a family richly blessed by cumulative good fortune.

"Late as usual," Connor Scott muttered as he entered from the living room. "Do you get the impression he just doesn't care about what's important to us?"

Connor was artistic, intelligent, and personable—a borderline nerd well-liked by his peers. Now in his senior year, he would soon graduate from high school. It was this accomplishment, plus his just-announced acceptance to college, that the family was supposed to be celebrating.

"Don't be snippy," Allison cautioned. "Your father works extremely hard. He has a great many responsibilities. Besides, he is an excellent provider."

"That kind of says it all, don't you think?" Connor turned around to address the family's six-year-old golden retriever, Torus.

The dog was on the verge of entering the formal dining room.

"Oh no, you don't. You can't come in, remember?" He chuckled. "You never give up, do you, old fellow?"

The dog halted at the threshold and lay down, his patient eyes fixed on his master.

Connor stepped around to the far side of the table and sat down in the straight-backed chair that faced his mother. Rather than brace his forearms against the table as was his habit, he folded his hands in his lap, waiting.

Allison smiled pleasantly. "I am so pleased you've decided to live at home—for your first couple years at least."

"I knew you would be," Connor admitted, affirming that his mother's sentiments had influenced his decision.

A mere fifteen-minute drive separated the Stanford campus from the Scotts' Menlo Park home—an easy commute even during rush hour.

The acceptance letter had arrived that afternoon, and while Connor's academic standing had virtually guaranteed his admission, his father's status as an alumnus had clinched the committee's decision. Still, the invitation to enroll as a freshman in the fall had come as welcome news indeed.

The vacant chairs that surrounded the table caused Allison to recall lavish meals served to distinguished guests, especially in the early years of their marriage when Reid was building his first corporation. Now the empty seating seemed nothing more than wasted space.

Where have those years gone? she wondered. *How did life become so solitary?*

Connor gave his mother an odd look. "How do you think Father would react if I were to choose graphic design as my major?"

"*Not business administration!*" Allison exclaimed. "I thought you two had settled that issue. Isn't that what you decided? Prepare yourself to take over his company?"

"*He* decided," Connor corrected. "As usual, I listened. So how do you think he would respond?"

A worried frown deepened the fine lines at the corners of Allison's eyes.

"That bad? That's what I figured."

A brooding silence fell over the room, the only noise being the ticking of the sideboard clock. Then came the sound of the garage door opening, followed by the Lexus's throaty rumble as Reid pulled in and parked.

Connor folded his arms over his chest. "Sounds like Daddy's home."

Reid descended the stairs, having hurried to his room to change out of his suit upon arriving home. He now wore a dress shirt with its button-down collar under his customary gabardine sweater. Dressing properly for dinner was a sign of good breeding. His hand slid along the solid oak banister.

Halfway down the stairs, he caught the scent of Cantonese food—one of his favorite cuisines. His wife, only a middling cook, must have ordered takeout from the Peking Lotus. Whatever announcement was forthcoming, it had to be important.

But then so was his.

Tangy aromas reminded Reid that he had skipped lunch, choosing instead to sharpen his wits for the contractual melee that lay ahead.

As usual, Reid found the table meticulously set when he entered the dining room. Tendrils of steam drifted up from a bowl of reheated white rice. He noted three covered dishes—their main entrées. One would be char siu pork with plum sauce and honey. Another was deep-fried chicken with sweet-and-sour sauce. As to the third, he would have to wait and see. It would be another of his wife's small surprises.

Allison and Connor were already seated at their usual places, their empty plates showing that they had waited as a sign of respect. The gleaming plates also stood as a subtle indictment. Being late for dinner demonstrated a lack of good manners.

Ah well, Reid consoled himself, *some transgressions can't be avoided, not if one hopes to put food on the table.* He considered offering an apology but feared it might be misconstrued as an indication that he could have rescheduled negotiations, which would have been unthinkable. *It's a matter of priorities*, he told himself.

After greeting his son and kissing his wife on her cheek, Reid took his place at the head of the table. Allison passed him the rice bowl. The family supper was officially underway.

A period of light banter ensued; banalities were easily forgotten. Weightier topics by tradition were avoided till the latter half of the meal. The most serious matters would wait until dessert had been served.

In time, Reid looked at his son.

"I understand you have an announcement—"

Connor started to respond, but Reid cut him off. "So do I. This is a red-letter day for our family. Or a black-letter day in terms of our bottom line." He chuckled.

"How splendid," Allison said brightly. For the second time, she offered her husband the platter of Peking duck, their third entrée. Reid shook his head, and Allison's smile vanished. "I thought you liked duck."

"I had a big lunch," Reid said gently. "Truly, everything was delicious. You've outdone yourself."

Allison aimed a cautionary look across the table at their son. "Connor, I think we should allow your father to go first. What do you say?"

"Why not?"

Reid noted Connor's reaction. He assumed the boy's displeasure sprang from having to wait to share his secret. Or perhaps he had guessed what was coming—another discussion centered on making money.

One day, the boy would learn. Hard work and dedication are how one affords the amenities that make life tolerable.

Reid sipped his green tea and then set the small cup aside. "I sealed the deal with Berlman Automotive this afternoon," he announced proudly. "The contract is signed and notarized. All that's left is to have our design team integrate the expanded reality module into their navigation software."

"Whatever that means," Connor muttered sourly.

Reid glowered at his son. "Someday hopefully you will understand exactly what it means and why it's important. This family's prosperity depends upon my ability to deliver a quality product. Keeping the company competitive is my responsibility, as someday it will be yours."

"I know, Dad. I get the message loud and clear. I got it the last time. I was only kidding, all right?"

"Were you? You should be thrilled that the contract is signed. Let me tell you, it was no mean feat. You would not believe the snags I had to overcome. It was one hurdle after another."

Connor seemed to shrink inside himself as if praying that the interchange would come to a swift conclusion. "I'm happy for you, okay? No doubt your efforts were impressive. They always are."

"You're damn right." Reid sat back. His hands gripped the armrests of his chair.

"Well now, that is wonderful news." Allison, always the peacemaker, again smiled sweetly. "I hope this means you'll spend more time at home now that the pressure is off?" She tilted her head ever so slightly.

Reid shifted his attention to his wife. Although not gorgeous per se, she had a pleasant face with features that complemented one another: the tapered eyebrows, the graceful chin, the flare of her nostrils, the way her cheeks dimpled when she smiled. Everything fit. His mood softened. "I promise. Tomorrow I won't be late for dinner."

Allison nodded and then looked across the table. "Son, I believe it's your turn."

The boy squared his shoulders and glanced at his father, but he then seemed to change his mind. "I'll be right back." He rose from his chair and hurriedly left the room.

Reid gestured to his wife in a way that asked, "What's going on?"

"I don't know," Allison replied aloud.

"What's this big announcement that's so important?"

"I think it's best if he tells you himself. Let's be patient and see what he has on his mind."

Connor returned with a drawing in hand, an image done with pastel pencils on sanded paper. It captured a sparrow in midflight illuminated by the rays of a setting sun. Every line was precise, the colors clean and vibrant. The boy crossed the room to stand beside his chair. "I finished it last night, but I haven't sprayed it with fixative yet. So please handle it only by the edges." He tentatively passed the drawing to his father. "What do you think?"

Reid accepted the drawing and studied it closely. "I think it's very good. Very good indeed."

"Mr. Tidewaller, my art instructor, says I have real talent." Connor sat down. "He told me I'm the best student he's ever taught. Can you believe it?"

"Judging by this," Reid said, "I certainly can." As cautioned, he held the drawing by its deckled edges.

"That's what I hoped you would say." Connor drew in a deep breath and cast a glance at his mother.

Allison scowled and mouthed the words "Not now."

Taken aback, Connor hesitated.

"What?" Reid said, still studying the picture.

Connor kept his eyes fixed on his mother.

Allison shook her head sternly.

"Well, eh—that is—" Connor stammered.

"Is what?" his father said.

"Well, do you think we could frame it and hang it somewhere in the house?"

Allison breathed a sigh of relief.

"Absolutely," Reid declared. "I'd be pleased to hang this in my den if you'd allow it."

Connor shrugged. "Sure. Why not? How about I give it to you for your birthday?"

"It would be my honor to accept it—if you're sure you want to do that."

"Then it's yours." Connor slumped back in his chair and folded his hands into his lap.

"This is your surprise?" Reid rose to gingerly lay the drawing flat on the sideboard. He turned and stood waiting.

"Go ahead, tell him the real news," Allison prompted.

In a matter-of-fact tone of voice, Connor said, "A letter came from Stanford today. They've invited me to enroll in the fall. I'm going to be a college freshman."

"My alma mater!" Reid exclaimed. "Fantastic. That is wonderful news. I have no doubt you'll do the family proud. Truly, this is a red-letter day." He returned to his chair to sit down.

"I thought you'd be pleased," Connor said, "with me following in your footsteps and all."

"You bet I'm pleased. This is a huge step forward. In no time, I'll be working with you at ERA. You know what? I've been saving this as a surprise for later, but since you've given me a gift, I should reciprocate. How would you feel about having your own car?"

"Seriously?"

"You bet. You'll need one if you plan on commuting to college." Puzzled, Reid studied his son. The boy's excitement was less than he had expected. Perhaps the significance of what was being offered hadn't fully registered.

Connor broached a smile. "Having my own car would be great. Thanks, Dad."

Torus materialized at the entrance to the dining room, having abandoned his bed in the family room. The dog began whining.

Allison took note and said, "I think someone needs to go out."

"I'll take him," Connor volunteered.

"Do you want company?" Reid suggested.

"There's no need. We can manage." Connor rose from the table and stepped around to where Torus waited, eagerly wagging his tail.

"Don't go far," Reid commanded.

"Just to Drystone Park. He can do with a little exercise." The boy reached down to scratch the dog behind his ear. "Can't you, old fellow?"

"Don't be gone long," Allison said.

"I won't. It's only four blocks. We'll be there and back in no time." Connor entered the kitchen to retrieve his navy-blue windbreaker and the dog's leash from the coat closet. He also grabbed a tennis ball off an upper shelf. Torus began prancing when he recognized his toy.

After clipping the leash to the dog's leather collar, Connor herded his charge out the front door. "We'll be back soon," he called out over his shoulder before heading off.

Reid waited until his son was gone and then rose from his chair. "I'll help you clear the table."

Allison stood as well and began stacking dinner dishes. "No need. I've got this."

Under his breath, Reid muttered, "Seems like nobody wants to share my company this evening." He flexed his back and glanced toward the sideboard. He stepped closer to inspect the image. "What was all that business with this drawing?"

"He wants you to be proud of him."

"I am."

"For the right reasons."

"Meaning what?"

Allison glided forward to touch her husband's face. "You're exhausted. I can see it in the way you move. Go in and get comfortable. I'll bring you some coffee, and we can talk."

Reid was forced to acknowledge that his wife's assessment was correct.

After a long, grueling day, he was too fatigued to pursue the question that had piqued his curiosity. He headed into the family room to prop his feet up and catch up on the news.

Reid lounged in his favorite easy chair, his feet and legs resting on the ottoman. Its corinthian leather gave off subtle creaks as he moved. His eyes scanned the headlines displayed by one of the half-dozen news apps he had installed on his Android tablet.

Although familiar with all things digital, he sometimes missed the congeniality of a daily newspaper. Except newspapers were slow. By the time the printed editions reached his doorstep, the world had moved on.

Allison entered the family room carrying two mugs of coffee. She handed one to her husband and then sat down in the rocking chair beside the gas fireplace—another amenity the family never used. She set her mug down on the side table and gathered up her embroidery. "That was wonderful news you shared at dinner. Convincing Berlman Automotive to sign must have taken a great weight off your shoulders."

"It did." Reid's eyes remained fixed on his news feed.

"I don't mean to pry," Allison said mildly, "and I appreciate that you would rather keep your business dealings private, but tell me, what is this contract worth to ERA?"

Startled, Reid regarded his wife with a penetrating stare. "Mostly it means that we can continue our research and development. This is our first venture into the marketplace. I'm surprised you'd ask."

"Sorry. I didn't mean to pry."

"No, it's all right. By now, you should know that it's not that I guard my privacy. It's that you've never shown an interest in our finances. If there's something you want to know, I'll tell you."

"Well, I was just wondering—when will it be enough?"

"When will what be enough?"

"Chasing wealth."

"Are you saying I'm obsessed with making money?"

"Aren't you?"

"Seems to me we've had this conversation before," Reid commented sourly.

"That's because the issue hasn't been settled. Tell me if you retired tomorrow, couldn't we live comfortably for the rest of our lives and never worry about money?"

"I suppose." Reid switched off his tablet and set it aside.

Allison's hand froze in the middle of setting a stitch. "I think I know what drives you. You view providing for our family as both an opportunity and a responsibility, but why insist that our son share your goals?"

"Does this have something to do with that comment you made about loving our son in the right way?"

"It distresses me watching you pressure him to follow in your footsteps."

"Does it? Perhaps I should explain why I feel the way I do. I've never worried about our son's ability to make money. He's bright enough to handle that on his own. What I want is for him to discover new things, to find solutions to problems that will enrich the world, to invent things no one has ever envisioned. Working at ERA would afford him that opportunity."

"Which is another way of saying you want him to carry on your legacy, to bear the Scott name and keep it alive."

"Of course I want that. Every father does. But that is not my primary hope. What I really want is for him to experience what I felt when I first realized what well-designed software can do—the exhilaration, the thrill of creating something out of nothing. It's hard to put into words, but that experience is what I crave for our son."

Allison lowered her embroidery to her lap. "Is it possible that he gets the same joy, the same exhilaration from his drawings? I mean, did you see his face? Did you notice the look in his eyes?"

"I saw his pride, yes, and I'll admit he has talent."

"He needs training."

"No doubt, but it's hard to make a living drawing pictures."

"You see, there's your mistake. It's not about making a living. It's about making a life."

Reid pressed an index finger to his lips. "Shh. Do you hear that? Sounds like something scratching on the front door." He rose from his chair and stepped into the front entryway. When he opened the door,

Torus bounded inside, his leash still clipped to his collar. The dog was alone.

Stepping out onto the front porch, Reid cupped his hands in front of his mouth and yelled, "Connor, you out there?" He paused to listen. No response. He called again with the same result.

"What could've happened?" Allison's voice was edgy with alarm.

Reid advanced to the sidewalk and called again. His eyes scanned the street in both directions. They waited for a time.

"Where could that boy be?" Allison said when Reid returned to the front door.

"I wish I knew," Reid replied sourly as he moved inside to grab his coat, "but I guess I'd better go find him."

Reid grabbed his jacket and a flashlight out of the kitchen closet. He thought about heading upstairs to retrieve the pistol he kept in the top drawer beside his bed, but then he told himself he was being paranoid. The dog had probably just run off. While Connor was looking for him, Torus must have decided to come home on his own. It had to be that simple.

Drystone Park was a modest-sized community facility about four blocks from the Scotts' home. It offered open spaces for sports and games, picnic areas with tables and firepits, and shaded paths for leisurely strolls.

Reid set out in that direction. His assumption was that Connor would not have altered his destination without alerting them first.

Light spilled out through the windows of all the houses Reid passed except for two. He tried to recall the names of the families who lived there, but he could not.

Strange, he thought. *I'm on a first-name basis with the janitors at work but can't remember the people who live a block from my front door.*

At the entrance to the park, Reid paused to listen. His flashlight probed recesses in the surrounding foliage for as far as its beam could penetrate. He then turned the flashlight off and waited until his eyes adjusted to the darkness.

A crescent moon overhead cast a yellow glow across the landscape. Peering into the dimness, he saw only vague shapes. Nothing moved. It seemed that the park was deserted. He switched the flashlight back on.

With deliberate slowness, he made his way through the picnic areas and scanned the open spaces. He checked the public restrooms, but no one answered when he banged on the doors. Again and again, he called out. His words trailed off into silence.

When Reid reached the far boundary of the park, he phoned home on the off chance that Connor might have returned via a different route. Allison confirmed that their son was still missing. Her voice communicated unmistakable apprehension. Calmly Reid reassured her that everything would turn out fine—a guarantee he himself was beginning to question.

The last place to look was the wooded trail that crossed the gentle terrain along the park's eastern boundary. He followed the asphalt path. Eucalyptus, pines, and an occasional live oak muffled the sounds of his footsteps and limited his visibility on either side. A gust of wind ruffled the fallen leaves. The flashlight's beam swung from one side of the path to the other in deliberate arcs.

Then there was a shape ahead. Reid froze in his tracks, his brain unable to process what his eyes were seeing. His flashlight illuminated a dark form beside the path thirty yards in front of him. He adjusted the beam and pointed the light directly at the shape while he stared intently, still unwilling to accept what was becoming apparent.

With slow purposeful strides, he advanced, keeping the light fixed upon his target. For a fleeting instant, he relaxed when it seemed that the shape was nothing more than a pile of rubbish.

An overturned trash can lay nearby. But as he drew closer, his apprehension flared with redoubled intensity. He thought he could see a limb sticking out to one side.

The breath caught in his lungs. His heart began to pound, each pulse thudding in his ears. His legs wobbled like columns of rubber that refused to bear his weight. From ten yards away, he knew he was looking at a body lying on its stomach. There was no doubt it was human, though the face was turned away.

Dear God, no! he screamed inside his head. The words ricocheted throughout his skull.

Upon looking more closely, the person's jacket seemed familiar. Still, his mind refused to acknowledge the truth.

He knelt and ever so slowly repositioned the head. The hair at the back of the scalp was moist and sticky. His fingers touched something squishy. Hastily he averted his face and vomited beside the path.

When Reid mustered the courage to look again, the flashlight's beam illuminated the unnaturally pale face of his son. A trickle of blood trailed down from a small dark hole at the center of Connor's forehead.

His most terrible fear had been made manifest. His only son, the heir to his fortune, the child who was to carry on the family name, was dead.

When the shock and disbelief began to fade, a flicker of hatred took root in Reid's heart. It quickly flared into a blazing fury that would become an unquenchable rage.

2

BEGINNINGS OF A SORT

Late July 1998

One month after earning a bachelor of arts degree in computer science from Stanford University, Reid Scott found himself in a narrow parking lot on the outskirts of Menlo Park. The Nobel Business Complex stood as a nondescript collection of freestanding office suites. The stucco-clad buildings seemed to glitter in the early morning California sunshine. On the surrounding surface streets, rush-hour traffic was thinning.

Reid's interest was centered on a vacant suite of four offices that also included a reception area, a private bathroom, and a utility closet. Like the adjoining rentals, the building was saddled with small thermal windows. At the front, a covered walkway connected each unit with the next. The rental's major appeal was that it was unoccupied, which suited Reid's purposes perfectly.

Gavin Marsh stood beside the friend he had known since high school. Uncertainty clouded his face as his dark eyes scanned the complex's unpretentious exterior.

Gavin was a humble man with a swarthy complexion. Reid had always assumed his friend had descended from Eastern European ancestry.

"You sure about this?" Gavin asked. "I mean, it doesn't seem especially grand, considering the lease payments they're demanding?"

Reid nodded. "If you're saying it's drab and ugly, I agree. But keep in mind it's all about location. Besides, for both of us, the daily commute will be a breeze. More to the point, we're fifteen minutes from the heart of Silicon Valley."

Gavin seemed unconvinced. "We should think about this—check other listings. Surely, there must be other office complexes that aren't as pricey."

Whereas Reid had chosen a career centered on creating software for the digital age, Gavin had majored in business administration. For him, the flow of money was always a consideration. Whenever his notable intellect grappled with thorny issues, one could trust that money would be part of the equation.

Reid glanced at his friend. "You worry too much."

Four inches shorter and thirty pounds heavier than Reid, Gavin more closely resembled a fullback than a quarterback, though neither man had opted to join Stanford's athletic programs, both being encumbered by nerdish tendencies.

Gavin laid a hand on his friend's shoulder. "One of us needs to. That's for sure. Seriously let's shop around and find something cheaper. Every dollar we don't spend on overhead helps. The longer we can go without income, the better our chances of success."

"Too late." Reid fished in his pocket for a matching pair of keys. He handed one to Gavin. "I signed the lease this morning. Phrase Systems is no longer homeless."

"Phrase Systems?" Gavin mused. "That's the name you picked for this adventure of ours? I like it."

"It seemed appropriate. Come on. Let's go in and look around." Reid unlocked the front door and stepped inside. Gavin followed.

The four office spaces were virtually identical, the only differences being the placements of the doorways and which walls housed the electrical and internet outlets.

After a brief inspection, the two men returned to the reception area where Reid faced his companion. "You get to choose." His arm swept the building's interior to indicate the available rooms. "Which do you claim as your own?"

"Actually," Gavin said modestly, "I was thinking I would put my desk there." He pointed to the north wall of the reception area.

"You're kidding?"

"It's a good choice for several reasons. First off, we really don't need a receptionist. We're not going to be that busy, not for months to a year at least. Besides, answering phones and greeting folks is easy. It won't impact my serving as your business manager in the least, and without a receptionist, we can hire a second programmer—part-time anyway."

Reid nodded thoughtfully. "There is that. I wish I had a better handle on how long it'll take to flesh out the algorithm. A third coder would surely help." A sense of uneasiness descended upon him as he recalled the final months of his third year in college during which he had experienced a sudden epiphany.

While enduring an esoteric lecture on optimizing the flow of digital information, a remarkable algorithm had popped full-blown into his head. In the space between heartbeats, he had visualized a new method for compressing text messages, thereby increasing transmission speeds by 30 to 50 percent. During his senior year, he had devoted himself to perfecting his idea and testing the algorithm as thoroughly as possible.

Reid looked around, suddenly aware that his dreams teetered on a knife's edge. In this suite of offices, he would either succeed or fail. This was where he would learn if he could incorporate his algorithm into modern telecommunication protocols. It would be from these rooms that he would reach out to the titans of the software industry—men who controlled the ebb and flow of digital information. Here, his future would be determined for either good or bad.

Gavin's brow furrowed. "Is there any word on your patent?"

"None yet."

"What's the holdup, I wonder?"

"Probably governmental bureaucracy. Besides, I'm not sure how long processing an application is supposed to take."

When Reid had eventually recognized the commercial value of his algorithm, it had occurred to him that it would be wise to protect his intellectual property. Three months before graduation, he submitted a patent application. Now there was nothing to do but wait.

"Without a patent, it would be insane to market—"

"I know that," Reid snapped.

"I'm sure you do." Gavin fashioned a worried scowl and then glanced around hopefully as if needing a place to sit might cause a chair to appear. When nothing materialized, he eased sideways to lean a shoulder against the nearest wall. "I think I've located a source for our furniture and equipment needs. Their prices are reasonable. How about you? Any luck on hiring a programmer?"

"Maybe. There was a guy who graduated a year ahead of us— Charlie Townsend. He's pretty sharp as I recall. I asked around. Word is he hasn't found work yet. I sent a text message. I'm hoping he'll get back to me soon."

"Townsend? Do I know him?"

"I'd doubt it. He pretty much kept to himself."

"A computer programmer who's been out of work for an entire year in Silicon Valley? How good can he be?"

"It's not his skills that are the issue. To say he's something of a slob would be like calling a lightning bolt a spark."

"Well, if you do hire him, make sure he bathes at least occasionally. By the way, does Allison know you've signed the lease?"

"She does. She's the one who convinced me to take the plunge."

"Brave lady. Does she also know about the mountain of debt we're incurring?"

"Not to the penny."

"That would be a no, I presume."

"I sort of implied that my father's inheritance would cover our start-up costs. She's comfortable with that."

"What do you think she'll do if and when she finds out?"

"She's not going to find out—not unless you tell her. Besides, a year from now, money will be among the least of our worries."

"Good lord, I truly hope you're right about that." Gavin's voice conveyed more than a hint of doubt.

"Look," Reid said soothingly to alleviate his friend's uneasiness, "if you're not comfortable with going ahead, feel free to back out. It's a huge risk we're taking, absolutely, and I won't hold it against you. When

I invited you to invest as a junior partner and take on the role of business manager, I made it clear that you could change your mind right up till the day we opened for business. Well, this is that day. If you're unsure, speak up now."

Gavin hesitated as if weighing his options. Pushing off from the wall, he thrust out his chest. "I'm with you. After all, what good is money other than for providing security, peace of mind, social status—the creature comforts that make life tolerable?" He gave a nervous chuckle. "Seriously, you think I'd bail out now? We've known each other forever. It's only right that we tackle this together. I'll be beside you to the bitter end or, if the fates are kind, to the glorious conclusion." He smiled with genuine affection. Then he bowed his head.

"What are you doing?"

"Praying."

"You really think that helps?"

"It sure can't hurt to ask the Almighty for a little assistance."

"Whatever."

When Gavin finished, he looked up and offered Reid his hand. "I guess this means Phrase Systems is officially launched."

"Right. You can begin tomorrow by drafting our articles of incorporation."

"Maybe the day after tomorrow. Tomorrow, I think I'll move in some office furniture, especially something to sit on."

Three years after launching Phrase Systems, Reid Scott found himself having to deal with a lawsuit that had been slowly working its way through the judicial system. The litigation had the potential to put him out of business.

Reid pulled into the narrow lot and parked. He had arrived at work early in anticipation of a stressful day.

The short commute from Atherton, where he and Allison lived in a one-bedroom apartment, had proceeded without incident, except for his having to contend with clogged thoroughfares.

This morning, however, traffic snarls were among the least of his concerns. Foremost in his thoughts was the deposition he was scheduled to give that afternoon. There was, however, one item of good news. The night before, he had finally located the document that could possibly save his company.

Still seated in his Subaru, Reid reached for the briefcase lying on the passenger seat. He exited the car and locked its doors. It was the same vehicle he had driven since his sophomore year in college.

When he entered Phrase Systems through the front door, he was only mildly surprised to find Gavin already at his desk in the reception area engrossed in what he was doing.

Gavin looked up with a startled expression. "Oh good, you're here. I've been jotting down some bullet points for you to touch on this afternoon. I'd like to go over them with you when you have a chance." Gavin combed his fingers through his wavy hair, which was already turning prematurely gray.

"Why? You worried?"

"You're damn right I am, and you would be too if you had any brains."

Challenging each other's intellectual abilities had become a standing joke between the two men.

"If Xadr succeeds in nullifying our patent, we'll be in a world of hurt. What time are you going in?"

"The deposition is it three thirty. I thought I'd leave around a quarter to two." Reid set his briefcase down on a metal-framed chair and stepped to the serving station in the corner.

Gavin had already made coffee. Reid helped himself to a steaming mug. Both men tended toward a strong dark brew. Reid turned to face his business manager and smiled.

Giving a snort, Gavin clearly articulated his opinion that his boss was being entirely too cavalier.

Ninety-three days after signing the lease and establishing Phrase Systems, the patent office had approved Reid's application. Reid knew it was exactly ninety-three days because he had nervously counted each one. Being granted a patent guaranteed that any use of his compression algorithm would be protected by the full force of United States patent law.

But then, nineteen months later, as potential clients were beginning to appreciate the worth of his algorithm, Xadr Software had filed a lawsuit challenging his ownership. The essence of their claim was that he had stolen their intellectual property, and therefore, the algorithm rightfully belonged to them.

Xadr had based their allegations on the fact that Reid had worked part-time as an extern during his senior year while participating in a work-study program.

Reid sipped his coffee and then stepped forward. He set his cup down on the reception desk and retrieved his briefcase. Opening it, he extracted a sheet of narrow-ruled eight-by-ten notepaper that displayed both text and hand-drawn sketches. He held it up. "I think this might bolster our defense a tad."

"What is that?" Gavin said skeptically.

"Last night, I was musing about the lawsuit and how to prove the algorithm is rightfully mine. After all, I'm the one who came up with the idea. I'm the one who fleshed out the compression methodology."

A worried frown darkened Gavin's face. "You do realize, I hope, that your having created the algorithm is not at issue. Xadr isn't questioning your authorship. They've already conceded it was your idea and that you wrote the code. What they claim is that you created the algorithm while working for them. According to the contract you signed, any salable idea that popped into your brain during your employment automatically became their intellectual property."

Reid gave his business manager a look of appeasement. "Of course I understand the nuances of intellectual property rights, and that's why this is going to save our bacon." He fluttered the piece of paper in his hand. "Last night, I was thinking about the moment when I first envisioned the algorithm. The idea sort of came to me in a flash all at once. It was during Harry Tuttle's lecture on the efficient transmission of information. Never had such a fully formed concept occurred to me all at once.

"As I was recalling that moment, I pictured myself jotting down a flow diagram so I wouldn't lose the thought. And realizing that, I went out to the garage and began rummaging through my old lecture notes."

"You kept your old lecture notes?" Gavin said with astonishment.

"You didn't?" Reid feigned a look of censure. "Anyway, after digging around a while, I found this." He handed the paper to Gavin. "Note, if you will, that the sketch in the margin is a flow diagram. It outlines the algorithm's core features. Also, notice the date at the top of the page.

As you can see, I jotted down those notes and drew that diagram four months before starting my externship at Xadr."

"This is fantastic!" Gavin exclaimed. After examining the paper a second time, he returned the document to Reid. He then leaned back in his chair and laced his fingers behind his head. Looking up, his grin abruptly disappeared and he sat forward. "I foresee a problem. Xadr's attorneys will claim you created this document retrospectively. They're going to challenge its authenticity. There's a good chance it'll never see the light of day."

"I thought of that. We'll submit it for chemical analysis. Tests will prove the ink used to draw the flow diagram is the same as the ink used on the rest of the page. Not to mention that I have an entire semester of notes written with the same ink.

"Professor Tuttle will confirm that my notes accurately reflect the substance of his lectures, proving I was in attendance. Therefore, the idea was mine, and I wrote it down three months before I started working for Xadr."

"Wow." Gavin took a moment to digest what he was hearing. "Are you going to show this to Xadr during your deposition?"

"No. First, I'll get it authenticated by a reputable lab. Then I'll give it to our attorney, and he can decide when and how to use it."

"Sounds good to me."

The phone rang. Gavin answered it as Reid headed toward his office. After listening briefly, Gavin called him back. He looked worried. "That was Allison. She's on her way to the hospital."

"She's not due for another week!" Reid exclaimed, as if his wife could be held accountable for going into premature labor. "Let me talk to her." Reid reached for the phone.

Instead of handing over the receiver, Gavin hung up the phone. "She said she couldn't wait. I think you'd better go."

Reid hesitated and then returned to his office to retrieve his briefcase.

As he strode toward the front door, Gavin blurted out, "What about the deposition? Want me to reschedule—family emergency?"

"No. We need to put this problem behind us. I'll work it out. Allison is tough. She'll probably be delivered by the time I get there."

"What's your best guess—boy or girl?" The Scotts had elected not to learn the baby's gender in advance.

Reid shrugged. "Seems like we're about to find out."

"If it's a boy," the business manager suggested slyly as his boss hurried toward the parking lot, "Gavin is a fine name—"

The flow of traffic leading into San Jose was light.

Reid arrived at the Thornwood Medical Center in near record time. The volunteer manning the front desk directed him to the labor and delivery suite.

At the nursing station, the ward secretary informed him that yes, he could see his wife, but only briefly since she was due to be taken into the delivery room. In addition, hospital policies required that all guests gown up before visiting patients.

After donning a paper gown, a paper bonnet with an elastic headband, and a pair of latex-free gloves, he was escorted into his wife's room. The antiseptic smell was even stronger there than in the corridor. Fluorescent lights overhead greeted him with an electric hum as he passed through the swinging doors. A series of squiggly lines trailed across the flat-panel monitor mounted at the bedside.

Reid tried to make sense of the numerals also displayed. He thought one grouping might be his wife's heart rate and blood pressure. The rest were a mystery.

Standing beside the vital sign monitor in a far corner, a nurse in paisley scrubs was keying notes into a tablet computer. She nodded politely to Reid before leaving the room.

In the middle of the room, Allison lay in a hospital bed. Her pale complexion glistened due to the perspiration on her forehead. Her shoulder-length hair, normally meticulously styled, lay spread out on the pillow in haphazard disarray like an auburn halo. An intravenous line fed fluid from bag on a tall metal stand into a needle in her arm. Another tube delivered oxygen through prongs in her nose.

As Reid watched, a spasm of pain contorted his wife's face. For a moment, he had the eerie sensation that his wife's suffering was his fault, which in fact was logistically true.

When the spasm abated, Allison glanced in his direction. "Nice of you to join us. I wasn't sure you would make it."

Reid stepped forward to gently grasp his wife's hand. Her skin felt clammy, but her nails were freshly manicured and painted with rose pink polish. "I told you to call me—that I would come get you and bring you in."

"I tried. You didn't pick up. When I couldn't wait any longer, I called your office."

"Damn. Last night, I must've been so distracted that I forgot to charge my phone. I am so sorry."

"Well, we're here now. That's all that matters." Allison forced a smile, but a fresh contraction short-circuited her effort. As it passed, she relaxed a little. "How did your meeting go? Did that paper you found make a difference?"

"The deposition isn't until three thirty."

"Hopefully we won't hold you up that long." Allison massaged her very-pregnant belly.

"Let's not worry about depositions, shall we? Has the doctor been in? Did he say how you're coming along?"

"I'm at eight centimeters. He thinks I'll reach ten in no time. He seemed surprised. I guess women who haven't given birth usually don't progress so quickly."

"You've always been exceptional."

Through clenched teeth, Allison groaned, "Flattery won't get you off the hook. I blame you for this, you know." Her gesture referenced the tubes and wires attached to her body. "Have you given any thought to the names we talked about?"

"I guess I like Erin if it's a girl—Connor if it's a boy. What do you think?"

Allison nodded. "Connor is a good choice, but I was thinking Aileen for a girl."

"Aileen is fine. I could go with that."

Reid studied his wife. She usually preferred not to be seen without makeup, but it wasn't modesty that he noted. There was something more. She seemed anxious, a little worried. Stress lines at the corners of her mouth heightened his impression. "You're going to be fine, you know. You're a strong, healthy woman, and you can do this—"

The monitor's buzzer began bleating. When Reid looked, he noted that one numeral on the screen had begun flashing red. What it signified, he had no idea.

In short order, a nurse surged into the room. Almost immediately, another followed. They stepped to opposite sides of the bed, displacing Reid as if he wasn't there.

The older nurse, who obviously was more senior, rapidly assessed Allison's condition. Taking hold of her wrist, she probed for a pulse. A moment later, she spoke to the junior nurse who had just silenced the alarm, "Call Dr. Blumefeld please."

The junior nurse hurriedly left the room.

Turning back to Allison, the senior nurse softly caressed her forehead and announced, "You're going to be fine, sweetie, but I think it's time for your baby to be born."

"What's happening here!" Reid exclaimed. "What's going on? Is she all right?"

"Your wife is fine, but we're seeing signs of fetal distress. We need to deliver your child now. If you would, do me a favor and go out to the desk. The ward secretary can show you to the waiting room."

"I want to stay with my wife."

"You'd only be in the way. The best thing you can do right now is trust that we know what we're doing. Please I need to get her ready for delivery."

Reid bent down and kissed Allison's cheek. "I won't be far. You hang in there. Remember, you can do this. I love you."

"I love you too." Once again, Allison tried to smile, but apprehension turned her expression into something more like worry.

"Is there anything I can do?" Reid asked.

"You can pray," the nurse suggested.

"I'm not a religious man," Reid said rather sheepishly.

"Perhaps now might be a good time to reconsider your theology." The nurse went back to caring for Allison as if her husband had ceased to exist.

As instructed, Reid set out to find the waiting room, his mind full of questions and his heart full of anxiety.

The well-appointed waiting room had comfortable couches that ran along two adjacent walls. One was long enough that a visitor might nap if so inclined. A line of armchairs fronted the opposite wall. There was even a high-back rocking chair with extra padding. A serving station in the corner offered coffee, tea, and fruit juices in individual cartons.

Looking out through the third-story windows, Reid faintly noted the southern reaches of San Francisco Bay in the distance. Rather than select one of the seating options, he had chosen to pace the length of the room repeatedly from entryway to thermal-paned windows and back.

Halfway through a transit, he paused to verify the time as displayed by the round-faced wall clock. Merely five minutes had passed since his last check. Twice in four hours he had returned to the nursing station to ask how his wife was progressing. On both occasions, the answer had been the same: "No word from the delivery room—we'll inform you of her condition as soon as we can."

A pudgy little man with a large bald spot at the crown of his head and a scruffy beard like steel wool lounged in an armed chair toward the far corner of the room. As if with nothing better to do, the man had been closely monitoring Reid pacing, his head swiveling like that of a spectator at a tennis match.

When Reid headed toward the windows again, the man nodded to himself and commented, "Now you take my missus for example. She's a trooper—pops them out without batting an eye. Yes, sir, a true baby machine. We have six now. This will make seven." Since entering the waiting room thirty minutes earlier, he had offered a dozen similar remarks.

Reid halted and turned to face the man. "Look, I know you're trying to be friendly. Maybe you're as anxious as I am, and jabbering is your way of coping, but you're not helping. So would you kindly shut up?"

The fellow recoiled. A crestfallen look spread across his face. "I meant no offense."

"I know," Reid said. "Look, I'm sorry. It's not you. It's just that I'm upset. I don't know if my wife—"

A figure in a white lab coat suddenly appeared in the entryway. Reid sensed his presence out of the corner of his eye.

He turned toward the new arrival. An older man with high cheekbones and a pinched nose stood peering at him through wire-rimmed glasses. Reid noted the name embroidered on the lab coat. It read, "Dr. Blumefeld."

"Mr. Scott?" the man said.

"Yes?"

"I'm your wife's obstetrician. I'm sorry we haven't met before. I'm a little surprised you chose not to accompany her when she came in for her office visits. Most husbands do, but then I guess with a company to run, time is precious."

"Indeed." Reid bristled at the implied accusation of indifference toward his wife's condition.

What stung even more was that the charge was essentially true. In fact, the Scotts had discussed what role he should play. Both had agreed that shepherding Phrase Systems through its legal crisis was as important as holding his wife's hand during her pregnancy. He was now beginning to sense that their choice had been wrong.

"What can you tell me?" Reid asked. "Is my wife okay?"

Dr. Blumefeld reached out to take hold of Reid's upper arm. "She's stable and resting comfortably. We have her in recovery. Why don't you come with me? There's a room down the hall where we can speak privately."

With a sense of trepidation, Reid trailed the doctor down the brightly lit corridor. They stopped in front of a door that bore the label "Chapel." The two men entered together.

Reid sat down in a chair like the ones in the waiting room. The doctor sat down next to him and leaned forward with his elbows resting on his knees. He let out a deep sigh and regarded Reid out of the corner of his eye. "How are you doing?"

"How do you think?" Reid snapped. "Sorry. I guess that pretty much tells it. Not having a clue as to what's going on is—"

"Nerve-racking?"

"To say the least. What can you tell me?"

The doctor rocked back and angled his body toward his patient's husband. "You should know that it's been nerve-racking for us as well. While you were with her in the labor room, your wife began having problems. There were signs of fetal distress. We can tell that's the case when the baby's heart rate begins to increase significantly. It turned out the cause was a placental separation. That's when the placenta prematurely tears away from the uterine wall. That causes less oxygen to be delivered to the baby.

"There wasn't time to let your wife deliver naturally. To save the baby, we were forced to do a cesarean section. That's a surgical procedure where we open the uterus and remove the infant manually.

"Everything was going well until we started to close. Suddenly she began bleeding uncontrollably. Our only option was to do a hysterectomy. That's where we remove the uterus and the fallopian tubes. The good news is we were able to save her ovaries. That will keep her from going through a premature menopause.

"Let me tell you, it was touch and go for a time, but when the bleeding came under control, things began to improve rapidly. She's doing well now, and I trust she'll make a full recovery."

"So she's okay?"

"Yes."

"Can I see her?"

"Soon." The doctor's demeanor became even more serious. "I'm sure you realize that hysterectomies are irreversible?"

"So?"

"Well, what it means is that your wife will never bear another child. She's permanently sterile. I am truly sorry. I don't know what plans you two had for a family in the future, but removing the uterus was the only way to save her life."

Reid leaned back and closed his eyes. He sat quietly for a moment as the implications of what he was hearing began to sink in. Then he opened his eyes and looked at the doctor. "But you said Allison is okay, right? And I can see her soon?"

"I'll take you to her now if you'd like." The doctor stood up.

Reid did likewise but found that his legs were a little wobbly. Jokingly he said, "This isn't the way I expected my day to go." Abruptly he recalled the deposition he had been scheduled to give. He could still make his appointment if he hurried.

For an instant, he felt tempted, but a deep sense of shame for even having had the thought swept over him. Instead, he would call Gavin and instruct him to reschedule the deposition. If his wife's surgery didn't qualify as a family emergency, nothing would.

The doctor laid a fatherly hand on Reid's shoulder. "By the way, congratulations! You're the father of a fine baby boy—six pounds eleven ounces. Because of the fetal distress, we were more than a little concerned, but as soon as your son was delivered, he began breathing on his own. And I can tell you he has a great set of lungs."

"I have a son," Reid whispered as he took in another dose of reality. "Connor," he declared firmly. "That will be my son's name. It's Irish, but we like the sound of it. It means 'wolf lover.'"

"Connor is a good name." Then the doctor suggested, "Let's go see your wife, and I'll introduce you to your son."

The two men left the chapel together to walk side by side toward the recovery room.

⁂

After again suiting up in gown, cap, and gloves, Reid was ushered into the recovery suite. Allison lay in a bed that paralleled the far wall.

The room's other three beds were empty. A plain white bedsheet and a thin blanket covered Allison from the neck down.

As Reid drew near, he again noted her disheveled hair. It bothered him only because she would never have allowed herself to be seen in public in such a state. Even more distressing, her complexion was paler than it had been before surgery. It caused him to wonder just how much blood she had lost. Filled with trepidation, he stood beside the bed.

Allison, apparently having sensed his arrival, turned her head slowly and regarded him with a drugged expression. Her eyelids seemed too heavy to remain open. "This is all your fault," she whispered, and then she drifted off.

Reid looked to the nurse. "Is she—"

"She's fine. There's still some anesthetic on board. She'll wake up in a bit. Oh good. Here comes your son." The nurse smiled in the direction of a stout woman who had just entered the room.

The second woman cradled a small bundle in her arms. When she advanced to where Reid was standing, he noted that it was a tiny infant she carried. A pale blue blanket swaddled the child. A knit skullcap rested upon the crown of his head like an oversize yarmulke.

"Normally we present babies to their mothers," the stout nurse said, "but she doesn't seem quite ready to receive her son. How would you like to hold him till she wakes up?"

"Sure," Reid declared despite his unmistakable misgivings.

With deliberate care, he accepted the precious bundle, the nurse making certain that the child was properly supported. Reid had the odd impression that he was holding a treasure made of the finest glass and that it might shatter at any moment.

"You'll get the hang of it," the nurse offered reassuringly. "They're more durable than you might imagine. Just don't drop him."

"I won't," Reid promised, mostly to reassure himself. He studied his son's face. "He's all wrinkled."

The stout nurse chuckled. "That's quite normal. He'll fill out over the next day or two."

At the sound of Reid's voice, the baby's eyes opened.

"Hello, Connor," Reid said gently. "Welcome to the world."

The first nurse touched Reid's arm. "You look a little unsteady on your feet. Are you all right?"

"It's been a rough morning, but I think I'm okay."

"Why don't we have you sit down? It may be a while before your wife is fully awake." The nurse urged Reid toward the gliding rocker on the opposite side of the bed.

After settling in, Reid felt his apprehension ease. As he regarded his son, the magnitude of the experience began to soak into his awareness. His thoughts were strangely drawn back to an earlier time.

Reid pictured himself leading a band of noisy hooligans across the spacious lawns of his father's estate. More than a dozen boys followed Reid's lead. Helium-filled balloons strained to break free from the tethers of ribbon that bound them to the chairs arranged near the main house. Crepe bunting dangled from the edges of the serving tables. Chinese lanterns hung from cords strung above the receiving station where the presents had been sequestered. Ewan Scott, Reid's father, had personally planned an elaborate birthday party. His only son was turning fourteen.

As he ran, Reid waved to his father, whom he noted watching from the back patio. Ewan's chest seemed to swell with pride.

Hickory-scented smoke drifted upward from the nearby barbecue. The master chef, especially hired for the occasion, made sure the hamburgers, hot dogs, and chicken breasts were cooked to perfection.

A treasure hunt had been arranged as the highlight of the festivities. Clues had been sequestered in diverse places across the estate's seven acres. Solving riddles to track down the treasure would take ingenuity and wit. Ewan seemed completely confident that his son was up to the task.

A lingering cloud drifted across the face of the sun. Ewan looked up.

Earlier that morning, the sky had threatened rain, but the storm had failed to materialize.

The afternoon was warming, but temperatures would remain well below the extremes of mid-July in Upstate New York. It was, all in all, a perfect day.

Shortly before the onset of World War I, Reid's great-grandparents had immigrated to the United States from Glasgow, Scotland.

Upon arrival, the family had changed their surname—Scott being far easier to pronounce than the Gaelic alternative.

Reid's grandfather had subsequently relocated to Lynchburg, Virginia. For a time, Ewan had lived near his parents even after his wife, Vera, Reid's mother, had died in childbirth.

After being promoted to regional vice president for IBM, Ewan had transferred to Ithaca, New York. His performance bonus had helped pay for the large colonial-style brick house with white shutters and doors, in which he and his son now resided. Their estate was only ten minutes south of Cayuga Lake.

From the direction of the gardening shed, a whoop of celebration rolled out across the lawn. Reid danced with glee. The knaves had found their treasure. Every child would receive a reward. The grandest prize was his of course.

In twos and threes, soon-to-be high school freshmen began returning to the patio, gifts in hand. Reid was among the last to return. Sensing a lull in the activities, he approached his father.

With solemnity, Ewan invited his son to step inside the house and led the way to the den, which was paneled in dark walnut and decorated with crests signifying the family's heraldry.

"I have something for you," Ewan said. "Something very special." He reached into the top drawer of his desk to fetch a finely crafted wooden box lined with red velvet. He handed the box to his son. "Open it."

Reid did so. Inside, he saw an ornate silver medallion. The boy looked up at his father in puzzlement.

Ewan tapped the lid of the box with his index finger. "Many generations ago, Robert the Bruce, king of Scotland, presented this medal to your ancestor Angus Straughan. It was to honor his conspicuous valor at the battle of Loudoun Hill in 1307.

"It's been in our family ever since. My father gave it to me, and now I'm giving it to you. One day, when the time is right, you will give it to your son. It's a reminder of our heritage." Ewan's mood became solemn as he looked at his son. "We have a sacred duty to preserve our honor and to share the love that binds our family. Do you understand?"

Holding the box carefully with both hands, Reid stared at the shiny medallion. "Yes, Father, I do. I will keep it safe."

"I know you shall. You are a good son."

Two months later, Ewan Scott died of a ruptured cerebral aneurysm. Reid was sent to live with his grandfather in Lynchburg.

A piercing shriek startled Reid out of his reverie. Connor's shrill cry signaled that he needed attention.

Healthy lungs indeed.

Reid looked to the nurse with a helpless expression that clearly communicated, "What do I do now?"

After drawing the curtain closed around the bed, the nurse moved to stand in front of where Reid was seated. "The poor darling is hungry. That's all. Let's see if your wife is up to the task." She bent down to proficiently scoop the infant out of Reid's arms. She then faced the bed and gently shook Allison's shoulder.

When Allison's eyes opened, she seemed less groggy.

The nurse smiled. "There's someone here who wants to say hello."

A gasp of astonishment escaped Allison's lips as she encountered her son for the first time. "He is beautiful. Is he—"

"Right as rain," the nurse announced. "Everything is where it's supposed to be—ten fingers, ten toes, two ears, a nose, and all the rest of the necessary equipment." After helping Allison expose a breast, the nurse laid Connor at her side to suckle. The shrill cries ceased immediately.

Reid had never watched a baby nurse before. He felt as if he should look away, but he couldn't. It was such an intimate tableau that the memory of it would never leave him.

"Do you still think it's my fault?" Reid asked to his wife.

"Yes, I do." Allison tenderly stroked the tip of a finger through Connor's downy hair. "And thank you so very much."

"No, thank you. You did all the work."

"Connor?" Allison asked, looking up at her husband.

"If you agree, that's what we'll name him."

"Connor it is then." Allison turned her face toward the nurse. "Did everything go okay? All I remember is being wheeled into the delivery room."

Soothingly the nurse said, "The doctor will be in to talk with you shortly. For now, let's just enjoy this precious moment, shall we?"

Two years and three months after Connor's birth, Reid lay in bed with his eyes closed.

It was a Sunday morning, and he had slept in. Rather than roll out of bed immediately upon awakening, he had lingered, comfortably lounging between satin sheets.

Allison's side of the bed was already growing cold. As usual, Reid's mind was dealing with business issues. More precisely, he was plotting how to boost Phrase Systems to even greater heights of prosperity.

Over the preceding eighteen months, the company's net worth had grown phenomenally. The compression algorithm had been successfully defended in court.

Xadr's claim of ownership had been soundly defeated. Two industry giants had signed highly lucrative contracts, incorporating Phrase System's software into their telecommunication packages. With the company's bottom line solidly in the black hefty bonuses had been paid to all employees.

When Reid opened his eyes, he was afforded proof of his newfound affluence. The master bedroom in which he lay was nearly the size of the apartment that he, Allison, and Connor had shared in Atherton. What was more, the Silver Vale House had four additional bedrooms, all nearly as large—Silver Vale being the name given to their new home because its address was 317 Silver Vale Court, Menlo Park.

The floor plan also included three bathrooms, a living room, a family room, a den, a more-than-ample kitchen, plus a four-car garage. Optimally positioned on an acre of land, the house was the most splendid thing Reid had ever dreamed of owning.

Even so, his home wasn't the grandest castle in the realm—a fact that offered a not-so-subtle comment as to the social standing of his new neighbors.

The stack of boxes sequestered in the corner of the master bedroom gave evidence that the house had not yet become a home.

Reid listened and heard faint sounds emanating from one of the rooms below him. He assumed Allison was busily completing the task of settling in.

He climbed out of bed and began his morning routine. When dressed in slacks, loafers, and a royal blue polo shirt, he made his way downstairs.

He found Allison in the kitchen standing near the sink. She wore a pair of faded jeans and a plaid cotton shirt, indicating this was a day for doing chores.

"Where's the little beastie?" Reid asked as he headed straight for the coffeepot.

"Still asleep." Without turning around, Allison inclined her head toward the baby monitor on the counter.

"How long since you last checked on him?" Reid poured himself a mugful and took a sip.

"Fifteen minutes. He's fine." Allison crossed to the stove. "This kitchen is gonna take some getting used to."

A complete set of new appliances had been installed immediately after the deed had been recorded.

"Everything is so modern."

She removed a kettle from its burner and drizzled hot water into a cup that already held a tea bag. She then turned to face her husband with a cheerful smile. "What would you like to eat? Waffles, French toast, scrambled eggs—your choice."

"I'm really not hungry. I thought I'd grab a bagel and cream cheese before heading into the office."

"Oh no, you don't. Today you're mine. First, we're going to sit down and have a nice breakfast—the first real breakfast we've shared together since moving in. Then you're going to help me unpack." She punched her fists onto her hips, a sign that she meant business.

"Perhaps this afternoon. I've had a thought on how to structure our sales—"

"No way, José. You are not about to shuffle off and leave me here to do all the work. Fifty guests will be arriving tomorrow night, and I expect this house to look presentable. Hosting a housewarming was your idea, remember? And you're the one who insisted that the party be as soon as possible. I mean, who invites a houseful of guests to drop in one week after closing? No, you're staying home. Now what do you want to eat?"

Meekly Reid conceded, "Bacon and eggs please." Taking his mug in hand, he sat down at the oval table in the breakfast nook and watched while Allison went about fixing their morning meal.

She moved efficiently and with grace despite having to cope with unfamiliar surroundings.

After setting out their breakfasts, Allison added toast, marmalade, and fruit compote; and she then joined her husband. As she salted her eggs, she said, "I hope some of the people you've invited eventually become more than acquaintances."

"Meaning—"

"It's time we had some real friends, I think."

"We have friends."

"We have people we know—not the same."

Reid counted off on his fingers. "There's Gavin and Frank—and Charlie, though I admit sometimes his eccentricities can be a bit daunting."

"Those are your friends. What friends do we have in common?"

"Well, there's—how about Dottie and Michael? They're good people."

"She's your corporate accountant. He's your fix-it man. I hardly think they qualify. I want people in our lives we can do stuff with, talk to—people whose company we enjoy, not potential clients you're trying to impress."

"Networking with the right kind of people is vital if a business hopes to survive."

"No doubt. And I don't begrudge you your professional contacts. What I'm talking about are people who have common interests, friends who are just friends and nothing more."

"What do you suggest?"

"Maybe we should join a church. Wouldn't that be a good place to meet nice people?"

Reid shook his head. "Churches are full of hypocrites who say one thing and do another. How about a country club? There's one less than a mile from here. I've heard it's rather nice."

It was Allison's turn to squash the suggestion. "Snobs and phony social climbers' frequent country clubs. I'm talking about real friends."

Reid chuckled. "Maybe that's why we don't have any. Our standards are too high. Look, I believe I understand what you're saying. Let me think on it. I'm sure we can figure out an adequate solution."

The front doorbell rang. Reid rose from the table and went to see who might be calling.

When he opened the door, he discovered Gavin Marsh standing a few paces back on the front walkway as if uncertain which entrance to use. "Servants around back, right?"

"Nonsense. No matter where we live, you're always welcome. As a matter of fact, we were just talking about you—sort of. Come in." Reid ushered his friend inside.

Over the years, the Scotts had become so accustomed to Gavin's presence that he was considered a member of the family.

"I'm glad you're here. Allison has some odd jobs that need doing. You can help."

"Oh goody." Gavin shed his windbreaker and draped it over the arm of the chair in the entryway.

Reid retrieved it, handed it back to his friend, and indicated a coat closet nearby.

"Moving on up, are we?" Gavin stowed the windbreaker on a hanger.

"Only until the place feels like home." Reid thrust his chin toward the doorway to the kitchen through which Allison could be seen seated at the small metal-and-glass table.

"I get you." Gavin glanced toward the formal dining room with its huge dark-walnut table. "At least you haven't become that formal."

"You hungry? You're just in time for breakfast."

"Why do you think I'm here? Where's the little tyke?"

"Asleep." The baby monitor in the kitchen began chiming softly. "Apparently, not any longer."

"Good. I was hoping he'd be able to play with Uncle Gavin."

"You know, if you wanted to, you could create one for yourself rather than repeatedly borrowing ours. The process isn't hard. I'm sure we could find someone to teach you the appropriate skills." Reid slapped his friend on the back. "Go on in. Tell Allison what you want for breakfast. I'll bring Connor down."

Reid bounded up the stairs two at a time while Gavin entered the kitchen with a famished expression that declared he was starving.

⌘

Toward the middle of the afternoon, Reid and Gavin decided to take a break. Most of the boxes had been unpacked. Only a handful remained.

The two men retreated to the den. Reid settled into the overstuffed lounger. Gavin opted for the plush couch.

Reid let his gaze wander around the room. Books were displayed on only a handful of shelves.

Most shelves were empty. Portraits, photos, and diplomas decorated the walls. The family's meager collection of mementos and memorabilia had been strategically placed. Even so, large empty spaces remained.

A sense of dejection overtook Reid as he surveyed his domain. "I thought our stuff would fill up the place. It seemed like so much when we packed it."

"Not to worry." Gavin leaned back with his fingers laced behind his head. "In a year or two, you'll be puzzling over how to get rid of things. The second law of homeownership states that stuff expands to fill the space available."

Reid chuckled. "So I've noticed. What's the first law?"

"No matter how diligently you maintain a place, there's always something to fix."

"That's for sure. Is there a third?"

Gavin grinned. "It's a corollary to the first law: Whatever needs fixing will always cost more than you expect."

"Splendid." Reid sighed, feeling suddenly downhearted. "Do you think I made a mistake buying this house? I mean, who needs five bedrooms when it's just the three of us?"

Rather than answer, Gavin shrugged in his own ineffable fashion. Over the years, Reid had learned it was his friend's way of avoiding expressing an opinion that might give offense.

"I was afraid you'd say that."

Gavin shrugged again.

A child's laughter floated in from the direction of the family room.

All morning, Connor had been helping his parents unpack. It was now Allison's turn to benefit from his efforts.

"As he grows, you're going to have your hands full," Gavin commented. "He's a bright kid with his own way of doing things. It'll be a challenge helping him reach his maximum potential without being overly domineering."

"I've noticed that already. I just wish I had more time to spend with him. He's usually asleep when I leave for work, and he's often in bed when I get home." Reid gave his friend a look of caution. "Don't say it. I know what you're thinking."

"Do you?"

"The problem is I'm responsible for the company's success. People depend upon me for their jobs. Without me, Phrase Systems would cease to exist. It's vital that I put in the hours I do."

Gavin sat up. "So it's a matter of setting priorities."

"Is it wrong to strive to provide a secure future for my wife and my son?"

"I didn't say that, but the better question might be 'How much is enough?'"

"Meaning what?"

"When is it safe to cut back on work and spend more time with the family? Perhaps the real trick is to recognize that moment when it comes."

"Perhaps. Speaking of families, did you know that Allison has been hinting that we should adopt a second child?"

"Really?" Gavin regarded his friend with interest.

"I'm sure you remember that she can't have any more children. I gather she feels—how should I say it—incomplete, diminished somehow—like she's letting me down."

"Have you two talked this over?"

"Not with words. It's a sensitive subject, but I've tried to reassure her as best I can."

"And how do you feel about adopting?"

"Raising a child is an amazing experience. It's both joyful and nerve-racking. But a second child, one who isn't biologically my own, the thought scares me."

"Scares you? Why?"

"It's a matter of emotional loyalty. I fear I would always favor my natural offspring. I'd advance his interests above those of any child that didn't share my DNA. I wouldn't want to, but I sense it's who I am—something to do with carrying forward the family genes and all that. But enough about my family. What about yours or the absence thereof? Seriously I've known you all these years, and you've never mentioned why you haven't married and settled down?"

"The truth?"

"Yes. I'd really like to know."

"I'm waiting for God to bring me the right woman."

"Well, that's a relief. Here I was, afraid you were going to tell me you were gay. Do you really believe God puts people together like He's some sort of heavenly matchmaker?"

"I believe God plays a role in every aspect of our lives."

"Well, I, for one, find it hard to imagine there is an almighty."

"How can you not believe in God? The evidence of His existence is all around us."

"What evidence?"

"The order and structure of the universe. The closer we look, the more intricate reality becomes virtually without limit. There is zero probability that anything exists as a by-product of random chance.

"The universe is simply too complex. Take your compression algorithm for example. Can you envision any scenario by which something so intricate might spontaneously spring into being? No. Your code is an existential manifestation of your intellect. You thought it, and it became real. Such is God's relationship with the world. He spoke us into existence."

"You believe God created everything that is?"

"Absolutely. Actually my reasoning goes like this: For lots of reasons, I'm totally convinced that we are created beings. And if there's a creation, there must be a creator. Logic also tells me that such a creator would have created everything around us."

"I'll admit I've never felt comfortable with the theory of evolution. I find it ludicrous to imagine that life is the product of a string of random events. But to claim that God is active in our daily lives, that's a stretch."

Gavin swept his arm wide, indicating the room in which they sat. "All of this—do you really imagine you acquired it solely by your own doing?"

"You're damn right I do. I worked hard for what I have."

"Indeed, you did your part. There's no question of that. But God allowed you to prosper for His purposes. My prayer for you is that someday you will discover what His purposes truly are."

Growing frustrated, Reid stood up. He had no wish to escalate their conversation into an argument. "Let's finish unpacking. Then we can see what new chores Allison has waiting for us."

"I meant no offense," Gavin said as he rose from the couch.

"None taken. You're too good a friend to let theological differences drive a wedge between us." Reid wrapped an arm around Gavin's shoulders and gave him a manly hug. "After all, who can know? Maybe you're right, though I really doubt it."

3

TOUGH TIMES

Late October 2001

A cold damp breeze rolled in off the southern reaches of San Francisco Bay. The air smelled of sea salt, diesel fumes, and the sandy marshes that fronted the national wildlife refuge across the bay.

Traffic along Pulgas Avenue—literally "the avenue of the fleas"—was sparse, as was to be expected at two thirty in the morning.

A crescent moon lingered overhead, barely visible through cracks between buildings. The city lights of East Palo Alto blotted out all but the brightest stars.

In an alley off the main thoroughfare, Maria Sanchez huddled beneath a pair of flattened cardboard boxes—one to cover her feet and legs and the other to cover her torso. Chilled to the bone, her limbs shivered and her teeth chattered, making sleep impossible.

On this, her second night as a homeless vagrant, the harsh severity of her predicament was rapidly becoming apparent. Unwashed, hungry, and afraid, the seriousness of her plight was compounded by the fact that, at seventeen, she was five months pregnant.

Maria rolled onto her side and drew her knees up to her chest, reducing the points of contact her body made with the frigid asphalt to as few as possible. She tried to ignore the other smells that joined those drifting on the breeze—rotting garbage and even less pleasant aromas.

The thin nylon windbreaker and soiled denim jeans she wore did little to shut out the cold, especially the chill that cramped fingers and toes. As she teetered on the verge of hypothermia, her thoughts were becoming scattered and diffused. She pictured herself lying in bed at home, warm beneath a wool blanket, listening to the sound of her younger sister's breathing.

But there would be no going home, no curling up in her own bed again, no lighthearted family reunion. Her stepfather had banished her, and being an incredibly stubborn man, he would never relent.

On her first day as an outcast, stunned by her exile, Maria had wandered aimlessly as she had struggled to cope. With what little money was in her pocket, she had purchased a single-serving yogurt on sale and a cheese stick. For a time, the meager fare had pacified her cravings, but then the gnawing rumblings had returned.

On her second day, she had tried panhandling. Inexperienced and mortified by her current state of being, she had attracted little sympathy.

After eight hours of begging, she had solicited less than $2.20. The scant amount of food she had purchased had again taken the edge off her hunger but had done little to ease her anguish. She figured that unless something changed radically, she would starve to death slowly.

Worst of all were the other denizens of the street and the way they treated her. As the newest homeless pariah, she was generally regarded as fresh meat.

During her first night on the streets while she was dozing fitfully, the backpack that contained the sum of her worldly possessions mysteriously disappeared. Twice, brutish men had displaced her from the sheltered recesses they claimed as their own. Three times she had been propositioned.

On the third occasion, she had seriously contemplated the offer. Only her pregnancy had prevented her from consenting. Unschooled in the ways of bearing a child, she had no idea what the sex act might do to her baby.

"Honey, are you okay?" said a woman's voice that came from out of nowhere. It was a soft voice, tentative and amiable, as if wishing to avoid giving offense.

Maria did not respond. Instead, she remained still, believing the question had come to her as a memory or a reverie experienced during the interval between wakefulness and sleep.

"I need to know if you're all right," said the voice again.

Maria slowly opened her eyes. Peering toward the entrance to the alley, she blinked several times as her vision adjusted to light given off by the street lamps.

A young woman stood facing her from several feet away. The woman, inclined forward at the waist, had her hands clasped together in a gesture of concern. As she appeared mostly as a silhouette, it was impossible to judge her features, though there appeared to be a golden glow around her head much like a halo.

For a moment, Maria imagined that the woman might be an angel come to escort her to heaven. But then she realized the halo was nothing other than light filtering through the woman's tousled blonde hair.

Maria also noted that she was wearing a robe and slippers—hardly the attire of an angel or a mugger for that matter. The realization caused her to relax a bit.

"I'm sorry to disturb you," the woman said, "but I couldn't sleep. I mean, I live across the street, and I saw you last night when you were checking out the alley. I suspected then you were planning on spending the night. When I woke up just now and saw you lying here—well, I must know if you're okay."

Maria sat up as best she could; her stiff muscles and joints were slow to respond. She cast a quick glance behind her to see if there was anyone else in the alley, and she then returned her attention to the woman. Through chattering teeth, she stuttered, "Who—who are you?"

"I'm sorry. I should introduce myself. I'm Caroline, Caroline Martin. Like I said, I live across the street."

"What do you want?" Maria shrank back against the brick wall.

"Nothing. I was just concerned. That's all. Look, I apologize if I startled you."

Maria tried to speak, but her mouth and lips were dry, and the words seemed to catch on her teeth.

"Excuse me?" Caroline said, taking one step closer. "I didn't quite hear that?"

Maria cleared her throat and tried again. "I'm cold."

"I can see that, you poor thing. Look, I live alone, and it's a one-bedroom apartment, but I got a real comfortable couch. You're welcome to use it for the night if you want. At least you'll be warm."

"You came out here to check on me?" Maria mumbled in disbelief.

"I couldn't sleep for worrying. It seems pitiful that someone should be in such a fix." Caroline eased nearer until she stood close enough to reach out and touch Maria's cheek. "Oh my gosh, you're absolutely freezing. You need to come with me right now. We'll get you warmed up." She offered a hand to help Maria stand.

Maria's survival instincts blared a warning, causing her to pull away, but then she asked herself a simple question, *Which is worse: being victimized at the hands of a stranger or freezing to death?* She allowed herself being helped to her feet.

When Caroline noted Maria's protuberant belly, she exclaimed, "Goodness, are you—"

"Five months," Maria admitted. A wave of embarrassment washed through her.

"And you're out on the street all alone. What is this world coming to? You come with me right now. We'll get both of you warmed up. And you look like you could use a good meal as well." Caroline wrapped an arm around Maria's shoulders and gently escorted her across the street.

In better light, Maria could see that Caroline was rather attractive. Strong cheekbones and sympathetic eyes complemented her well-formed lips and nose.

"What's your name?" Caroline said as they entered the apartment building.

"Maria."

"That's a pretty name. I had a cousin named Maria. She passed away when she was seven."

"So young. That's very sad."

"I know. She was a sweet girl."

Ascending the stairs to the second floor took a little more effort, but upon reaching the landing, the two women were greeted by a gush of warm air. For the first time since being cast out of her stepfather's house, Maria felt the spark of a new emotion, one she barely dared to acknowledge—hope.

Three months after being rescued, Maria stood at the sink in Caroline's small apartment. When she finished washing the last of the few dinner dishes, she set it aside in the drainer to dry. Their meager meal had consisted of nothing more than potpies and one bagel each, but at least the fare had been filling. She dried her hands on a paper towel and stepped into the living room that was also her bedroom.

She passed by the mid-century modern sofa that opened up to serve as her bed. Upholstered in blue velvet, its faded cushions were more comfortable than they appeared. As had become her custom upon arising that morning, she had neatly folded the bed linens and stashed them out of sight.

Maria approached the window to gaze out upon the fading twilight. Across the street, she noted the entrance to the alley from which she had been rescued. Seeing it rekindled memories that sent a cold shiver racing along her limbs.

The sound of a couple arguing filtered in from the apartment across the hall. Maria tried not to listen. She was beginning to suspect that the newlywed couple had made a huge mistake in getting married.

Why can't people simply get along? she wondered.

Suddenly she recalled the row she'd had with her father and his near-maniacal rage. The images were painfully vivid. She cringed and tried to refocus her attention.

There were noises coming from the bedroom where her roommate was changing out of her workday attire.

Upon returning home that evening, Caroline had seemed upset. When pressed to share her feelings, she had refused and instead had changed the subject by complimenting Maria on how neat and orderly the apartment now looked.

In the days immediately following Maria's rescue, the two women had discovered that they truly enjoyed each other's company. Rather than limit her hospitality, Caroline had invited her guest to stay on indefinitely.

In the first weeks, Maria had landed a few odd jobs, but as her pregnancy had progressed, finding even the most menial employment had become nearly impossible.

The arrangement the women had finally settled upon was that Caroline would pay the bills and Maria would do the shopping, cook, and keep the apartment neat and clean.

At about the same time with Caroline's help, Maria had enrolled in Medi-Cal, California's health insurance program. Knowing that it would help cover the costs of her pregnancy and delivery had lifted a tremendous weight from her shoulders.

Caroline emerged from the bedroom wearing a pair of khaki cargo pants and a mist green cotton blouse. Her hair had been pulled back into a short ponytail, and her makeup was gone.

Even so, she was still attractive. Maria pictured her own plain face and the dejection she felt whenever she regarded herself in the mirror.

"How was work?" Maria asked as she turned around and headed for a corner of the couch.

"Brutal. You want a drink?" Caroline halted abruptly on her way to the kitchen. "Sorry. Force of habit. How about coffee? Maybe a cup of tea?"

"Tea sounds nice. Let me get it. You come sit down. You look worn out."

"Perhaps so, but I'm not the one who's three weeks away from giving birth. You stay where you are. I can manage."

Maria did as instructed and gratefully folded her hands over her swollen belly. As she watched Caroline putter in the kitchen, she wondered what the woman's life had been like when she had lived alone.

There had been at least two boyfriends she knew about and perhaps several others before that but none in the last three months.

Why is the woman still single? Maria wondered.

Caroline was attractive, well-mannered, and easy to talk to. What was the problem? She wanted to ask, but she refrained. As a guest, she had no business intruding into matters that were probably none of her business.

Maria gratefully accepted the cup of tea that Caroline carried into the living room.

The ice cubes in Caroline's glass of bourbon clinked as she sat down. She leaned back, closed her eyes, and, crossing her ankles, stretched her long legs out in front of her. "How are you doing?" she asked, keeping her eyes shut.

"I'm good."

Caroline opened her eyes and sat up slowly. "There's something I'm curious about but we've never discussed. If you don't mind me asking, why did your father kick you out? You seem like a sweet girl. Look, you don't have to tell me if you don't want to."

Maria stiffened. "He said that I brought shame to the family that I had dishonored him. He called me a whore—a slut. He claims to be Catholic, but I don't think that's the reason. I think he was afraid of having another mouth to feed. He doesn't make much money, and he drinks up most of what he earns. Having a baby in the house would have been very hard on him."

"So the brute kicked you out. How cruel. Is there any chance you and he can reconcile?"

"None."

"Would you be willing to try if the opportunity arose?"

Maria thought for a moment and then said, "I am never going back. He did things to me when I was a girl. I'm done with him."

"Sorry. I didn't know that. What about the baby's father? Have you heard from him?"

"Not a word."

"Do you know how to get in touch?"

"I don't."

"Why did he leave? Was he afraid too?"

"As I said, my dad was furious. He told me that because I was underage, he was going to call the cops and have Duane put in jail for rape. I told Duane. The next day, he was gone. He never even told me goodbye. I miss him. He was such a beautiful boy." Maria gave a self-conscious laugh. "I think that's why I got pregnant. When he smiled at me, I couldn't keep my knees together. Why are you asking all these questions?"

Rather than answer directly, Caroline said, "Is the baby still active?"

"Sometimes it feels like he's jumping on a trampoline."

Caroline chuckled but then became more serious. "Have you decided what you're going to do?"

"About what?"

"With the baby—after he's born."

"You're asking if I'll put him up for adoption?"

Caroline nodded and then sipped her bourbon.

In response, Maria sipped her tea. "I thought about it—a lot. I don't know what to do. I don't know if I can give him away."

"You're seventeen. What will your life be like with an infant to care for? How will you provide for the two of you?"

Maria tilted her head and, with a puzzled expression, looked directly at her friend. "Are you about to tell me it's time for me to leave?"

"No, no, that's not where I'm going, at least not in the way you think. Maria, I do have something I need to share with you." Caroline downed a large swallow of her drink. "I've been offered a promotion."

"That's wonderful," Maria said with true joy, though she felt uncertain as to why her friend should seem so troubled.

She knew Caroline worked as a sales rep for a major pharmaceutical firm. On occasion, she'd been required to spend a day or two away while traveling. Beyond that, she had no idea what the woman's job entailed.

"You should be happy."

"I am for myself, but there's a problem."

"What sort of problem?"

"They've offered me a regional vice presidency. It's in the Midwest. If I accept their offer, it means I'll have to move. I won't be able to keep this apartment."

"Oh, I see." Maria rested her teacup on the shelf of her pregnant abdomen. "This sounds like a good thing for you."

"It will be a major promotion with a substantial increase in salary."

"Then you should definitely do it," Maria declared emphatically. "You've been more than kind. I know I can never repay your generosity. Taking me in like you did, it's—I don't have words."

"It's been a pleasure for me as well."

"When does this happen?"

"That's the good news. We have a month. I'll be here for your delivery. Look, I've gotten in touch with a residential women's pregnancy center. Usually they prefer to have their clients move in before delivery, but I explained your circumstances. They said they'd be willing to offer you a place to stay for a month or two after you have your baby. That will give you at least a little time to get on your feet."

"Thank you for all you've done. We'll be fine, me and the baby."

"I have no doubt. By the way, have you decided on a name?"

"Ruben James Walker."

"Not Sanchez?"

"Walker is his father's family name. Besides, I will never give my father the satisfaction of knowing that his grandson bears his name."

"Now *that* I can understand." Caroline slapped a palm flat on her thigh. "I have an idea. Tomorrow is Saturday, my day off. We should go shopping. There are lots of things you're going to need. Tomorrow would be a good day to get them."

"I can't afford to go shopping."

Caroline grinned. "I can. After all, I'm about to be promoted."

The sound of someone crying awakened Ruben Walker from his fitful sleep. He lay still for a moment. When he cracked his eyes open, he discovered it was still the dead of night.

City lights cast a pale glow through the grimy bedroom window. He listened intently to the soft sobbing, trying to pinpoint its point of origin.

Odd nocturnal noises often disturbed the impoverished neighborhood in which he lived. Most were full of anger or discord, but mournful sounds laden with despair were heard nearly as often.

The weeping that had aroused him had seemed different. He had the impression it was coming from within the cramped apartment.

For a scrawny kid, six-year-old Ruben was surprisingly self-reliant. Graced with a quick wit and a healthy intuition, he was better suited to be left on his own than most children his age.

Having survived in a tough neighborhood, he was already familiar with the ways of the street. Even so, the anguish apparent in the crying frightened him, though he would never admit it. Tears of sorrow meant someone was suffering and that someone had gained entry to their apartment.

Rolling onto his side, Ruben scanned the dimness for his two-year-old brother, Travis. The child appeared to be asleep. The thin sheet that covered his small body rose and fell with each respiration. The mattresses upon which the children lay had been placed perpendicular to one another on the floor so they could converse each night before drifting off.

For some odd reason, Ruben recalled the last conversation they'd had that night. Travis had asked why his last name was Zeller and not Walker or Sanchez like their mother's. Ruben had done his best to explain, but the toddler's mind simply wasn't prepared to contend with the dynamics of sequential paternity. Instead, Ruben had reassured his brother that they had different last names so Mama could tell them apart. The ruse had worked, and Travis had happily descended into slumber.

A heavy sob jerked Ruben back to the present. Noiselessly he rose from his mattress and padded quietly to the bedroom door to listen. Clearly, the crying was coming from within the one-bedroom apartment. He eased the door open and peered through the narrow crack. His mother lay curled up on the divan, her back to the wall, a towel held against her face. An occasional moist cough punctuated her soft sobs.

The cold towel felt numbingly good against Maria's swollen cheek. The blow would undoubtedly leave a bruise, but the mugger's fist had missed her eye socket. She rolled onto her back to stare at the ceiling, blinking several times to reassure herself that her vision was unimpaired.

Stupid, she thought. She should have seen the attack coming. How dumb not to notice a thug loitering in the shadows.

She blamed herself as much as she blamed her assailant, thinking that people who live in rough neighborhoods should expect to occasionally get roughed up. At least she had managed to keep hold of her purse and the money it contained—money she'd just been paid for working her second job.

Maria's daily grind had become an endless treadmill of struggle. Arising at 6:00 a.m., she had to hurriedly prepare Ruben for school and Travis for day care. After dropping the kids off at their respective destinations, she then would take a twenty-minute crosstown bus ride to her main job.

Working in a garment factory had its benefits and its drawbacks. The workload was steady, but supporting two children on minimum wage was nearly impossible. Plus, dust from the automated looms was hurting her lungs. Her cough was getting worse. Twice the EPA had threatened to shut the factory down.

After leaving her primary job at 5:00 p.m., Maria would ride the bus home. She would then retrieve Travis from day care and Ruben from Mrs. Robinson's house.

Mrs. Robinson, whose son William was Ruben's age, was a kindhearted lady and wholly aware of Maria's plight. Since she lived nearby, she had agreed to babysit Ruben after school. When Maria could afford it, she repaid the woman's kindness by baking a pie, sweet rolls, or such.

With the kids fed and settled in the apartment for the night, Maria would then change clothes and rush to board a different bus to reach her second job by 7:00 p.m. Only a month earlier, she had hired on with a downtown janitorial service. She liked cleaning offices and securing a second source of income had been a godsend, though she hated leaving her kids alone at night.

Upon finally trudging back to her apartment after midnight, Maria would normally fall quietly into bed and be sound asleep by 1:00 a.m. Five hours later, the cycle would begin anew.

This night, however, her tearful homecoming was not silent, nor was she able to fall promptly asleep.

A soft creak alerted Maria. She turned her head to look toward the bedroom where the children slept. The door was ajar. Out of habit, she had checked it upon returning home.

One of the boys was awake. She sat up and dried her eyes with her towel. "It's okay," she whispered softly. "You can come out."

Ruben emerged wearing only white cotton underpants. He looked to be mostly elbows and knees. His dark brown hair was a disheveled mess. As he padded barefoot across the floor, he seemed to be on the verge of tears.

"Don't be frightened. Mama's okay." Maria opened her arms and gathered her son into a tender embrace. The side of her face ached, but she smiled nevertheless.

"What happened, Mama?" Ruben asked.

Maria gave her son a loving squeeze and then invited him to sit down on the divan beside her. She hugged an arm around his shoulders, drawing him close, as much to comfort herself as her son. "A bad man attacked me, but I'm okay. I screamed and fought him off. You would've been proud. He didn't take our money. He was probably a druggie or one of those gang members who are moving into the neighborhood." She angled her body to look down at her son. "You need to promise me that you'll stay away from those guys. They are very bad. I don't want you having anything to do with them. You understand me?"

Ruben nodded.

"I want to hear it. Promise me. Do nothing with the gangs, okay?"

"I promise."

"Is your brother all right?"

"He's asleep."

"I haven't told you lately, have I? I'm very pleased with you and the way you look after him. You're a good brother." Maria had repeatedly emphasized that with Lincoln Zeller, Travis's father, being gone, Ruben was the head of the house and was therefore responsible for his sibling's welfare.

Ruben hesitantly reached up to touch his mother's bruised cheek.

Maria drew back reflexively. "It's nothing, just a little tender. I'm pretty sure it won't turn into a black eye."

"Who hit you?"

"I didn't recognize the man. I barely saw his face. I don't think he was from around here."

"I'll find him, and I'll kill him," Ruben declared flatly.

"Ruben James Walker," Maria exclaimed sharply, "don't you dare talk like that!" She drew back her arm from around her son's shoulders. "Vengeance is not ours to give. Remember?"

"He hurt you."

"Yes, and someday he will be judged but not by us." Maria vividly recalled the doctrines Caroline Martin had stressed during their brief time as roommates. "We forgive our enemies. Do you understand?"

"You believe God will punish the man?"

"Maybe not right away, but eventually, yes. I do."

"Good. But if God doesn't, I will."

After administering another stern scolding, Maria sent her son off to bed and then lay down to rest. In five hours, a new workday would begin. She had to be ready.

⁕

A noxious layer of smog had settled like a blanket over East Palo, though it might soon dissipate.

The evening rush hour was ending, and traffic was sparse along the populated corridor that stretched from San Mateo to San Jose. What's more, a faint breeze was sweeping in off the bay. Even so, the foul air stung Ruben's eyes as he escorted his eleven-year-old brother, Travis, home from school.

The two children trekked a convoluted route, avoiding areas of heavy gang activity. Their destination was the neighborhood day care facility where their twin siblings, Felicia and Davon, spent their days.

At two years of age, the twins' last name was Lane; and like their older brothers, their father had deserted the family soon after Maria had become pregnant.

Now fifteen years of age and a freshman in high school, Ruben regarded himself as the man of the house. The welfare of his sister and two brothers was his responsibility, and he took his duties seriously. As often as possible, he hustled odd jobs to help out, mostly on weekends but sometimes after school.

Once, he had tried his hand at managing a paper route, but local gangs had made his life miserable, stealing his money and trashing his undelivered newspapers. Another time, he had signed on to distribute political leaflets door-to-door with equally disastrous results.

Walking side by side, the brothers passed in front of the local pawnshop. Items displayed in the window caused Ruben to recall occasions when his mother had hocked this knickknack or that small appliance to raise money to pay the rent. He glanced down at his younger brother and wondered if he too shared the shame of those moments.

Never a talkative child, Travis seemed more sullen than usual. Ruben wondered if he had landed in trouble at school again. It was as if the kid had a knack for pissing people off. A rude remark would evoke an angry retort, and before you knew it, he'd be duking it out with some dude twice his size. More than once Ruben had soundly trounced his brother's tormentors, making it abundantly clear that Travis was to be left alone.

In front of the neighborhood butcher shop, Ruben halted abruptly. Placing the palm of his hand in the middle of his brother's back, he hustled him away from the doorway. "Wait here, and keep your yap shut."

Travis began to respond, but Ruben silenced him with a scowl.

After peering inside and confirming that Mr. D'Angelo the butcher was away from his counter, Ruben crept through the door, keeping his body low so as not to trigger the electric eye that announced the arrival of new customers. Moving noiselessly on tiptoes, he crept around behind the counter, all the while keeping a wary eye on the door that led to the back room.

Beyond the door, he could hear a soccer match being played out on television. The butcher was an avid fan and tried never to miss a game.

When Ruben reached the display case, he slid open the rear glass panel an inch at a time. Reaching in, he selected two of the choicest cuts of top sirloin. He then rearranged the remaining slices as best as he could in hopes of concealing his theft. Were he to abscond with more than two cuts of meat, Mr. D'Angelo would surely notice.

After silently sliding the case's back panel shut again, he helped himself to a square of butcher paper before leaving the shop. Hastily darting around the corner and out of sight, he wrapped the slabs of meat in the heavy brown paper.

Travis followed. "What do you think you're doing? You know how Mama feels—"

"She doesn't need to know. The thought of leftover tuna casserole makes me want to puke. Look, I'll tell Mom I found ten dollars on the sidewalk with nobody around. I searched but couldn't find the owner. It seemed a shame to leave the money there and let somebody else claim it. She'll believe me if you back me up. Do you really want tuna fish again tonight?"

Travis shook his head, though his reluctance was evident.

Ruben knew it was a dicey thing, pitting sibling loyalty against the risk of getting caught lying to Mom. He just had to trust that his brother would back his play. "Come on. Let's get the twins."

Ruben stashed the stolen meat in the refrigerator as soon as the four of them made it home.

Maria returned home from her day job at her usual time. Peering out of the grimy window, Ruben watched her step off the crosstown bus a block down the street.

As usual, a cadre of women and several men joined her. There were nods of acknowledgment and a few parting farewells, but most of the commuters seemed too fatigued for extended conversation.

Ruben tracked his mother as she walked home. Twice, she paused to catch her breath. It troubled him that she moved more slowly than other women her age.

The previous month, he had broached the subject of her health. Her reply had been so harsh that he had not dared to visit the topic again. He listened to the sound of his mother's footfalls on the stairs and to her raspy breathing.

As usual, when Maria entered the small apartment, she dropped her purse on the floor by the chipboard end table that the family had purchased from a neighbor for two dollars. The twins were first to reach her, toddling eagerly into her open arms. Travis was next. Ruben held back while he mentally reviewed how he would approach the subject of the pilfered meat.

"How are my darlings?" Maria let out a sigh of relief as she sat down at the apartment's only table. The twins climbed onto her lap, one on each leg. Travis sat down facing her. She looked at Ruben. "What? You're not glad to see your mama?"

Ruben stepped forward to give his mother a kiss on her cheek. "Of course I am. How was your day?"

"Same as always." For a brief interval, she seemed lost in thought.

"I have a surprise, Mama!" Ruben exclaimed. It seemed best to jump right in to the matter rather than stress over how his presentation might go. He entered the small kitchen and opened the refrigerator to retrieve the package of meat. He laid it on the table and undid the coarse brown wrapping to expose the steaks.

Maria's eyes widened. "Where did these come from?"

Ruben launched into the story he had so carefully concocted. Maria listened closely. When her eldest son finished, she looked at Travis. "Were you with him when he found the money?"

"No, ma'am." Travis locked eyes with his brother. "But he told me that's what happened."

"I see." Maria stood up and faced Ruben directly. "Explain to me again how you happened to come by two beautiful cuts of meat?"

Ruben looked away, unable to ignore the guilt creeping into his soul. Almost verbatim, he repeated the tale he had memorized. During the telling, he found it virtually impossible to maintain eye contact.

Maria's face hardened into a mask of indignation. "You're lying to me. You didn't find any money, did you?" She pointed to the steaks. "You stole these. That's what happened. Tell the truth. If you don't, your punishment will be very bad."

"I found—"

The slap came from out of nowhere so quickly that Ruben had no chance to prepare. It struck his cheek and spun his head to the side. The stinging began immediately and grew more intense over time.

"The truth!" Maria shrilled. "Don't lie to me again."

Tears welled up in Ruben's eyes. Never had his mother used physical violence against him. Yet the pain of her disapproval hurt worse than the impact against his cheek.

"I'm sorry, Mama," he wailed. "I was only trying to help. I thought you'd be pleased." At his mother's insistence, he described what had truly transpired.

Maria fetched her phone from her purse to check the time. She then carefully repackaged the steaks in their brown paper wrapping.

After retrieving her purse and the package of meat, she grabbed Ruben by the ear and marched him toward the door. "You're coming with me. If we hurry, we can just make it. D'Angelo closes at six." Before slamming the door behind her, she leveled her scowl on Travis. "I'll deal with you later."

When they reached the sidewalk in front of the butcher shop, Maria fished in her purse for her only ten-dollar bill. A few ones remained. She handed the money and the package of meat to Ruben. "Go in and do what I told you. I'll not have a son who is a thief and a liar. You admit what you've done and make it right."

"Mama, we can't afford these. That's why I took them."

"I'd rather spend every penny I own than have my son live without honor. Now you go in there and tell D'Angelo what you did. If he calls the cops and has you arrested, it'll serve you right. If you go to jail, I won't bond you out. Now go."

Ruben did as his mother had commanded. To his great good fortune, the butcher was a charitable man and treated the incident as a normal sale.

On their way home, Maria demanded to know what, if anything, her son had learned. His first inclination was to mention that he needed to become a better liar. Yet rather than reignite his mother's anger, he told her what she needed to hear that stealing was wrong and so was lying.

As Maria's wrath eased and the stress of recent events wore off, her fatigue became even more obvious.

Several times on the way home, she had to stop and rest. Once, it was more than a minute before she could catch her breath. When they returned to the apartment, Ruben was obliged to help her up the stairs.

Two months later, Maria Sanchez disappeared without a trace. A thorough search was conducted as was a detailed investigation, but she was never found. Foul play was considered possible but unlikely since no body was discovered. No evidence was unearthed to support the various other theories. Rumors spread of course, but the circumstances of her disappearance were never explained.

As the grief of losing his mother became less immediate, Ruben found himself in a very bad situation. He had become the head of his household for real, and his siblings' survival was entirely upon his shoulders.

4

PRIORITIES

Early November 2012

Ten years after purchasing the Silver Vale House, Reid Scott sat in this office at Phrase Systems and stared at a silver-framed picture of his wife and son. At thirty-four years of age, Allison was still quite attractive, but she had recently begun manifesting the effects of time's passage: crow's-feet at the corners of her eyes, strands of gray at her temples. And though only twelve, Connor was showing clear signs of having entered puberty.

Reid felt a pang of concern. Despite his best efforts to protect his family, recent events that were still unfolding had the potential to cause them significant distress. Yet the risk that Connor and Allison might be emotionally wounded by schemes that were now afoot seemed unavoidable, even inevitable.

Reid leaned back in his swivel chair. As his gaze traveled around the room, he noted photographs and mementos. Each artifact marked a milestone achieved or an accomplishment mastered. Such were the baubles that tracked his fourteen years as owner and CEO of Phrase Systems.

He shut his eyes and brought to mind various obstacles overcome and catastrophes managed or even avoided. Perhaps events rather than things would stand as a better yardstick by which to gauge his stewardship.

In truth, growing a company from scratch had proven exhilarating, but regrettably the journey was nearing its end. He opened his eyes and rocked forward. Hopefully his next adventure would prove equally stimulating.

Again, Reid slowly scanned the room. The built-in bookcases, the blonde wood paneling, the view through the panoramic windows, and even the square footage of his corner office gave testimony to the corporation's success.

Four years previous, Phrase Systems had relocated. After moving closer to downtown Menlo Park, the in-house computer systems had been substantially upgraded. A dedicated meeting room had been outfitted with all the necessary amenities. As they were no longer cramped in a small space, additional personnel had been brought in.

Phrase Systems now employed five full-time computer programmers and two system analysts. Reid recalled how pleased his business manager had been to finally hire an actual office receptionist. No longer was Gavin responsible for answering the phones.

A familiar knock sounded at the door.

Speak of the devil, Reid thought.

Gavin entered without waiting to be invited as was his custom. The two friends had known each other long enough that formalities were to be shunned whenever possible.

"What's up?" Reid asked.

Gavin seemed troubled. "Got a minute?"

"That depends. Are you the bearer of good tidings or bad?"

"I'm not sure. You're going to have to tell me." Gavin settled into one of the two armchairs that faced Reid's desk. Rather than rest his back against the padded cushions, he sat forward as if ill at ease. "There's an ugly rumor going around. I wouldn't bring it to your attention except I've now heard it from three different sources. I need you to tell me whether it's true or not."

"Let me guess what you've heard. People are saying that Allison and I are in the midst of a nasty divorce, and Connor is the subject of a vicious custody battle? Am I correct?"

"That sums it up. Please tell me this rumor is nothing more than vile slander, malicious gossip spread by our corporate enemies?"

Reid rose from his chair and stepped to the window. Gazing out at the cityscape, he clasped his hands behind his back. "Is that all you've heard?"

"Isn't that enough? What are you saying that there are other slurs out there?"

"So you're not aware that people are saying I've made some truly horrendous investments, and Allison is determined to take me for whatever's left?"

"Please tell me none of these rumors are true."

"I have many things I need to tell you, but not here." Reid turned around and smiled at his friend. "Are you hungry?"

"What?"

"Do you like Cantonese? A new restaurant recently opened across town. They make a great beef chow fan—that's beef with noodles. It's nearly lunchtime. What say we go there?"

"Forget lunch. I want to know what's going on."

"And you shall, but be patient. Besides, I really do have a hankering for Cantonese food. Grab your coat. I'll meet you in the parking garage. And by the way, don't mention where we're going. If anyone asks, tell them a client called, and we're on our way to sort out his concerns. I wouldn't want the wrong people to overhear what I have to tell you."

Gavin gave his boss a troubled scowl that clearly demanded an explanation.

"Bear with me," Reid pleaded. "There's more going on here than you know. Now act like nothing's happened. I'll be waiting in the garage."

After Gavin departed, Reid moved to his desk and pressed a concealed button, turning off the jamming equipment he had recently installed to prevent eavesdropping.

Its sophisticated circuitry was designed to ensure that privileged conversations, like the one he'd just had with Gavin, would remain private. He then quietly stepped into the corridor and more loudly returned to his office.

"If she thinks she's going to take me to the cleaners," he brashly said to the empty room and to whoever might now be eavesdropping, "she's dead wrong. Now get out. I don't want to talk about this. In fact, I think I'll take the rest of the day off." He then slammed the office door shut behind him as he headed toward the parking garage. He hoped any snoop would conclude he or she had been listening to the tail end of a conversation that had begun elsewhere.

The Peking Lotus was modestly busily when the two men arrived. They were promptly seated at a table toward the back of the restaurant. Paper lanterns hanging from the ceiling infused the interior with a pale yellow glow. On the walls, oversize hand-drawn portraitures depicted ancient Chinese warriors in heroic poses. A spicy aroma filled the dining room.

In the mood to try something different, Reid ordered wonton noodles and roast pork. Gavin selected chow mein and Cantonese shrimp. Both dishes included white rice and a fortune cookie.

"Nice place," Gavin observed as he sampled his entrée. "I'll have to remember to come here again."

"Allison and I chanced upon it about a month back," Reid said. "It was the week after its grand opening."

"Speaking of Allison—"

"I know." Reid set his chopsticks down on his plate. "I promised you an explanation, and you shall have it. But first, I need to tell you a story."

"As a rule, I'm not a big fan of stories. Am I gonna like this one?"

"That depends on how you feel about the effect fathers have on their sons. Once, there was a young boy about eight years of age. He lived with his father in a small southern town. His mother had died while bringing him into the world. So it was just the two of them—father and son.

"The father was a meticulous man, careful in all his ways. He seemed to prosper at whatever he set his hand to. Being something of a perfectionist, second best was never good enough. His obsession for success permeated everything he did. The problem was that it also carried over to his relationship with his son.

"One summer, the boy decided he wanted to enter the local Soap Box Derby. He was excited to compete because even relying on gravity, the cars could sometimes reach speeds of thirty-five-mile per hour or more.

"Anyway, the boy worked all summer crafting his car. He studied the designs of previous winners. He researched the best type of wheels to use and the best axles, making sure everything was as friction-free as possible. He shaped, sanded, painted, and polished his car until it was a work of art. He was very proud of what he had accomplished.

"Then came the day of the race. The boy easily won his first heat and his second and then the quarterfinals. When he also won the semifinals, he was absolutely elated. All the while, his father watched and made no comment at all.

"At last, it was time for the final race—the event that would crown the champion. Emotions were high, and the crowd was enthusiastic loudly cheering their favorite on.

"At the starting line, the boy's stomach was tied in knots. This was the first time he had attempted anything so public. While he and his rival waited for the gun that would launch them to victory or defeat, he could hardly control his shaking hands.

"And then they were off slowly at first but with ever-increasing speed as they rolled down the inclined racecourse. It was nip and tuck, first one car ahead by a few inches and then the other. The lead passed back and forth several times, but when they crossed the finish line, the boy had lost by the slimmest of margins. He had come in second. The winner's trophy was awarded to the other kid.

"On the drive home, the boy's father remained completely silent. He never spoke a word about the race. Not then, not ever.

"The boy understood that he had let his old man down. He had lost. He had failed at what he had attempted, which in his father's eyes was the gravest sin he could have committed.

"The boy learned his lesson well. He promised himself he would never fall short again. From that day forward, his highest priority would be to succeed no matter what."

During the storytelling, Gavin had forgotten about his lunch. When he recalled where he was, he took a bite of shrimp and then said, "You've never mentioned your father before. Why now?"

"Because it will help you understand what I plan on doing."

"And just what might that be?"

"I'm going to sell Phrase Systems."

"Why, for heaven's sake? Our balance sheet is in the best shape it's ever been. The economy is strong. Our customers are happy. Why would you want to bail out now?"

"Because the future looks grim. I've read the handwriting on the wall."

"What are you talking about? Our financial projections are solid. I've run the numbers myself."

"I know, but we're a one-trick pony. The compression algorithm is our entire product line. The lease agreements on our software are our only source of revenue, and that's a problem.

"On my flight back from Omaha last week, I was fishing around for something to read. By chance, somebody had left a copy of an obscure mathematical journal in the seat pocket in front of me. Out of boredom, I picked it up and began reading.

"Toward the back of the magazine, I found an article written by a Czechoslovakian mathematician, a guy no one has ever heard of.

"In the article, he lays out the fundamentals of a new encryption methodology. It took a while to work through the implications, but when I did, I could tell that we're in serious trouble.

"When his theories become commercially available, and they will, the telecoms will have a method for compressing their textual communications as efficiently as we do now and with equal speed.

"More than that, the transmissions will be encrypted. It won't take long for the industry to adopt this new technology. In a year, two at the most, our revenue stream will be bone-dry.

"And that's why I told you the story. I have no intention of sitting by and watching the company I so carefully built slowly fall to ruin."

"So we're going to sell, but to whom?"

"To Xadr Software."

"You're kidding."

"I'm not. They've been a thorn in our side since we began this venture."

"Why would they be interested in buying our patent?"

"Two reasons: First, despite their best efforts, they've never been able to produce a product as good as ours. They're determined to be the dominant player in the telecommunications arena and, by any means necessary, as they have so clearly demonstrated. Second, they are under the impression they have an opportunity to buy our company at a deep discount."

"Why would they think that?"

"Because they're under the impression my position as CEO has been weakened by recent developments."

Gavin's eyes widened in a flash of insight. "The rumors."

"Precisely."

"Then they aren't true?"

"No. They are not. My marriage is stable, and I'm nowhere near facing financial ruin."

"If that's the case, who's been spreading these lies?"

"I have."

"You? Why would—oh—you want Xadr to believe we're vulnerable."

"Bingo. And the plan appears to be working. Just this morning, a tender offer came in from Xadr's attorneys."

"For how much?"

"One hundred twelve dollars per share."

Gavin's brow furrowed. "That's a 20 percent discount from our most recent appraised valuation."

"That was their offer. We will settle for $120 a share. Even at that price, Xadr will imagine they're getting a great deal."

Gavin closed his eyes while running numbers in his head.

Reid could see where his friend's thoughts were headed, so he decided to save him the effort. "What this means is that after you exercise your stock options, you'll walk away with a little over $1.4 million—other employees with somewhat less. I'd say that's not a bad return for fourteen years' employment."

"Not bad at all," Gavin agreed with a nod. "What about you? I know you. You won't be happy without Phrase Systems to manage. What will you do with your time?"

Reid took a last bite. After wiping his mouth, he set his napkin aside. "That's where things get interesting. I recently became aware of a small start-up with offices on the northern edge of Mountain View. They've been in business for less than a year, and I happen to know they're hurting for cash. They're still in R and D and haven't yet developed an income stream. The company is called Expanded Reality Applications or ERA Inc. I plan on buying them out."

"Do they know you're interested?"

"We've been in touch. I gather they might be receptive to an offer."

"What do they do?"

"In a nutshell, they make it possible for people to experience the world around them more fully. It's somewhat akin to Google Glass but with different hardware and a vastly superior interface. Fundamentally they're an information storage and retrieval service. The key is that they've developed a slick method for dynamically recording the world as people experience it."

"What makes them unique?"

"Did you know that our country is on the verge of a transportation revolution? Self-driving cars will be a fact of life within the next five years. As the industry stands now, people will key in their destination and then sit back with nothing to do till they arrive. What I propose is to use ERA to make their trips more enjoyable.

"Imagine the possibility: If your vehicle is equipped with a Wi-Fi connection, you can retrieve information about any business, building, landmark, geological formation, social activity, or anything else you happen to pass along the way. Advertisers will jump all over this. They'll have a captive audience for the duration of the trip.

"Besides, the possibilities for social and business interactions will be almost limitless. You can have face-to-face conversations without worrying about reaching your destination alive."

"What about our other employees? What will happen to them?"

"I'm hoping that you, Charlie, and Russell will come with me. I need your business savvy, and they are excellent programmers. The others will get generous severance bonuses and strong letters of recommendation. I'm assuming Xadr will hire many of them."

"Sounds like you've thought this through."

"This means a new start, a chance to succeed all over again. What do you think? Are you in?"

It took Gavin less than ten seconds to make up his mind. "If you believe it's a good idea, I'm for it. You haven't led us astray so far."

"Excellent. I hope you understand you can't mention any of this to anyone, including Allison and Connor."

"What if they get wind of the rumors? Won't they be worried?"

"It's a risk I must take. It's vital that Xadr thinks I'm on the ropes. If their suspicions are aroused, they'll back out of the deal altogether."

"Surely there must be other potential buyers?"

"None I want to stick with a dying company. Xadr has earned this honor. This is my revenge."

"Remind me never to get on your bad side," Gavin said.

"Not to worry. I only screw my enemies." Reid grabbed the bill and started to slide out of the booth. "Lunch is on me. Come on. You need to get back to work, and I need to meet with the folks at ERA. We still have a ton of hurdles to overcome."

Gavin remained strangely silent during the ride back to Phrase Systems. He kept peering out of the car's window as if imagining what an enhanced drive might be like with reality augmented by a vast informational database.

Several months after Phrase Systems was sold to Xadr and Reid took possession of ERA, a new crisis arose to beset the Scott family.

The windows in the dining nook at the Silver Vale House offered a splendid view of the fenced-in backyard. Reid sat at the oval table, staring out at an expanse of professionally groomed lawn. The kitchen clock above the induction range told that it was a quarter past two in the afternoon.

Connor was now officially four hours overdue. Both Reid and Allison were growing increasingly worried, and so was Torus, judging by the way he looked around as if searching for his missing master.

At Allison's insistence, Reid had taken off from work at noon. The expanded reality project was entering a critical testing phase, and he had felt a great need to remain at ERA. Allison's premonition that something was amiss had finally convinced him to come home.

Connor had spent the night with a friend. The two boys had planned on going for a short sail that morning on his friend's sloop, and in fact a phone call to the boy's parents had confirmed that they had departed from the Sand Dollar Marina a little before 8:00 a.m. That was the last anyone had heard from either one of them.

The marina itself was nestled in a secluded harbor that opened out onto San Francisco Bay—an ideal place for two young sailors to practice their craft.

Connor, being a novice, would never have been permitted to take a boat out on his own, but his friend was an experienced seaman. It had seemed an ideal opportunity for Connor to learn something about watercraft.

"Try him again," Allison demanded nervously.

"It's only been ten minutes," Reid replied.

"Maybe they were out of range and now have reception again. You know how it is out on the water."

"Actually I don't, but if you think it's worth a try, I'll call." Reid speed-dialed his son's cell number and again was transferred directly to voice mail. He shook his head. "Want me to try the harbormaster again?"

"No. He promised he'd call as soon as there's news." Allison rose from the table and began pacing. She stopped to look at her husband. "I think it's time we notify the coast guard."

"Are you sure? The boys are probably having a great day on the water and have simply lost track of the time."

"And if that's not the reason they haven't checked in—"

After considering the issue, Reid consented, "I'll make the call." He stepped out of the room, ostensibly to fetch the guard's emergency contact number.

In truth, he wanted to speak privately with whoever answered the phone, just in case the guard had already received notification of a boating accident or other calamity.

He returned ten minutes later. "They haven't heard a thing, but they promised they'd alert their patrols to be on the lookout for a sloop in distress. All we can do now is wait, I suppose." What he failed to tell his wife was that he had been advised that a strong weather system was rolling in.

There was a wind alert for all of San Francisco Bay and the surrounding communities.

Four hours later, there was still no word. Reid had contacted all of Connor's friends—the ones he knew about at least. Not one of them had any information to share.

He had checked with emergency rooms in the area even as far north as San Mateo. No sixteen-year-old males had been admitted within the past twenty-four hours.

He had also received the same response from the police and sheriff's offices. No accidents involving minors had been reported. The other boy's parents were equally in the dark and equally worried.

"I can't just sit here," Reid announced. "I'm going to the marina. I want to be there when the boys return—" He refrained from adding "if they return." "Do you want to go?" he asked instead.

Allison nodded but then changed her mind. "I'd better stay by the phone in case someone calls. Be sure to let me know immediately if you hear anything."

"Don't worry. I will." Reid grabbed his coat and stepped out into the fading twilight.

The drive to the Sand Dollar Marina took all twenty minutes, but they were the longest twenty minutes he'd experienced in many years.

En route, his mind began to bring back memories of his son: his birth, his first bicycle, his Little League home run, his first day of high school. As he searched for other memories, he soon realized that the experiences he'd shared with his son were surprisingly few. They just hadn't spent that much time together.

A horrible realization descended upon Reid as he pulled into the parking lot at the marina. This day, if he were to lose his son, he would have precious little to remember him by. They had lived together but were only remotely connected. They had led separate lives. They had experienced milestones as individuals, not as father and son.

A frigid wind was howling in off the bay. Reid halted and stared at the water beyond the moorings. A terrible realization had thudded into his consciousness. He was treating his son the same as his father had treated him with cool indifference. The insight pierced Reid to the core of his being.

After twenty minutes waiting on the dock, a small coast guard cutter pulled in. Reid hurried to greet the vessel as it moored. He called out to the *Spearfish*'s captain before the man could step ashore. "Any word?"

"You mean about the missing sloop?" the man called back. "No. Sorry."

When he drew near, Reid noted that his name tag read "Jamison," and he wore the naval insignia of a commander.

Commander Jamison looked to be thirty something and athletically built. He shoved his hands into the pockets of his tightly zipped windbreaker. "We've been searching but had to come in. A crewman broke his arm—had to get him to the hospital. Two of our boats are still out there, but it's a mess. These gale force winds have been kicking up. Makes it hard to see past the chop, not to mention the darkness. I wish we had more of a moon."

The news deeply unsettled Reid. Rough seas, he imagined, could be a major problem—one they didn't need. Then an idea struck him. "You mentioned chop? What kind of problem does that cause?"

"It's not a navigation issue. We can hold a steady course in weather far rougher than this. The trouble is the waves are three to six feet high, and they all have white caps, and they're all over the place. The froth makes it hard to see anything in the water."

Reid thought for a bit. ERA Inc. had recently launched an R and D study to see if getting rid of motion artifacts could improve data collection. The project was showing promise but was nowhere near being ready for commercial use.

Turning to face Commander Jamison, Reid said, "I think I might have a way to help you. I own a small software company. We're working on expanded-reality applications. What we do is collect information about the environment that's all around us. We then translate that information into viewable objects on specially adapted displays.

"A problem we've had from the beginning is dealing with moving objects, such as cars and pedestrians. They get in the way of static structures, such as buildings and landmarks. We've been working on a method to filter out the noise and see only the fixed objects. A capsized sloop might fit that category."

"What are you suggesting?" Commander Jamison seemed strongly interested.

"Our techs use helmet-mounted cameras linked by Wi-Fi to servers in our labs located in Mountain View. We apply a proprietary data-reduction methodology that digitally eliminates objects in nonrepetitive motion. This enhances our view of stationary structures.

"The only requirement is that two or more cameras must be looking toward the same field of view. The cameras have a range of up to half a mile, and we can adjust for ambient lighting. If two boats were to track a parallel course up and down the bay, something floating in the water might be made visible even at night. And I just happen to have two helmets in my car. We were planning on doing a field trial this afternoon."

"Might be worth a shot," Commander Jamison said thoughtfully. "At this point, there's nothing to lose. If this wind keeps up, finding a small vessel like a sloop will be impossible. Get me the helmets, and I'll pass them to the other boats on the bay."

"Good. And I'll head to the lab. I can monitor their activities from there. I assume the captains have cell phones."

"They do."

"Excellent. I'll open a com channel as soon as I get to the lab. It might be best if the captains begin searching just north of the marina and follow the currents up the bay."

"That's what I was thinking."

After handing over the helmets, Reid headed for ERA at breakneck speeds.

For more than an hour, Reid had been guiding the search, instructing the captains on the best course to follow to maintain an optimum field of view. Eliminating wave patterns was proving to be more difficult than anticipated.

Apparently, ocean waves were not as random as they appeared. However, after fine-tuning the digital filters, he had reduced movement artifacts to a minimum. Yet there was still nothing to see, and he could tell the captains were beginning to consider his assistance a waste of time.

"Gentlemen, one more sweep please—a thousand yards east."

"Sir, we searched that area earlier," protested the voice coming from Reid's cell phone.

Twenty minutes earlier, his phone had died suddenly but had been immediately resurrected. Fortunately, ERA Inc. owned an abundance of USB chargers.

"That was before we began filtering the optics digitally. Let's give it a try, shall we?"

"Sir, I don't think—"

"It's my son who's missing. Humor me, okay?"

There was a long pause, and then the voice said, "Very well, sir. Heading to new coordinates."

Reid leaned forward to peer doggedly at his monitor. The view was somewhat confusing because he was looking at two images that were digitally superimposed. Even more frustrating was that there were few, if any, points of reference. All he could see was an inky black ocean on an inky black night.

Ten minutes later, a flash of white caught his eye. The glimpse was so fleeting that if he had blinked, he would have missed it.

"Captain," Reid bellowed into his cell phone as he stared intently at the screen, "have your crewman pan his camera twenty degrees west slowly." He exclaimed, "That's it. There! Do you see it? Looks to be about a hundred and fifty yards out. There, there it is again!"

"We don't see anything."

"Trust me. There's something out there. It's thirty-five to forty degrees left of your current course."

Reid watched excitedly as the cutter slowly came about. The view kept shifting, and for a time, he lost his bearing. Then he heard the words he had so urgently prayed to hear: "We see it. It looks to be a capsized boat or something of that size. Hold on."

The waiting seemed interminable. Then came the announcement: "There's movement. It appears we have two individuals clinging to a hull."

Only when the cutter had his son and his son's friend safely on board did Reid allow himself to relax. He immediately called Allison to share the excellent news that the boys were suffering from dehydration and moderate hypothermia but were otherwise unharmed.

Surrounded by a roomful of soulless machines, Reid leaned back in his chair and closed his eyes. His son was safe, and that was all that mattered. Or was it?

As he mentally dissected the day's events, it dawned upon him that he'd been given a second chance, an opportunity to make a new beginning.

He opened his eyes and peered around the room. He was alone. Bathed in the glow of fluorescent lights overhead and with only the quiet hum of the servers for company, he promised himself that he would better manage his priorities. No longer would his son be the second most important thing in his life.

The following March, Reid was seated in ERA's conference room. He glanced at his cell phone, which was lying on the large mahogany table. Its always-on display informed him that the contract negotiations had now been underway for more than six hours, though it felt like sixty, and he was exhausted.

Anthony Fox, Berlman Automotive's lead attorney, had doggedly raised one sticking point after another. Deftly each had been overcome. An end to the bickering and wrangling was finally in sight.

From across the conference table, Gavin Marsh looked to where Reid was seated and silently mouthed a question. Reid shook his head and held up three fingers.

"I'm afraid that doesn't work for us," Gavin told Mr. Fox. "We will need at least three months to complete the integration."

Mr. Fox, a wiry, ostentatious man, consulted his team and then said, "Very well. Three months it is."

And that was it.

Reid stood and flexed to ease the kink in his spine. "Gentlemen, thank you. It appears we have a viable contract. My secretary is already typing up the revisions we've agreed to. After we sign the appropriate documents, we can be on our way. My wife expected me home for dinner an hour ago."

After shaking hands all around, Reid left the conference room to return to his office. Forty minutes later, he was navigating surface streets along the northern edge of Mountain View. On his way home to the Silver Vale House, he thought about the evening ahead and how his son would react to learning that his father had just saved his company from financial ruin.

Of late, Connor had been distant, sullen, and withdrawn. Something was obviously troubling the boy.

Reid suspected he had an inkling as to what the cause might be. Not every son longs to follow in his father's footsteps, but then not every seventeen-year-old knows what's best. The boy would come around in time. Such was Reid's fervent hope.

For the last six months, Reid had made a determined effort to get to know his son and spend time doing things with him. However, fulfilling the promise he had made to himself was proving difficult.

Changing entrenched attitudes is never easy. Having grown accustomed to an arm's-length relationship, Connor had resisted his efforts. In addition, as a teenager on the verge of adulthood, Connor was beginning to exert his independence.

Still, Reid knew it was up to him to strengthen the bonds that joined them. How sad would it be, he wondered, if his son were to grow up with the same sense of estrangement he had gleaned from his own dad. How sad for a man to gain the whole world and lose his family.

These and other matters were on Reid's mind as he pulled into the garage at the Silver Vale House. He switched off the Lexus's engine and hurried upstairs to change clothes before dinner.

Despite the tension that permeated the formal dining room, Reid did his best to savor the Cantonese entrées.

The evening was unfolding as he had envisioned. Allison was pleasant as always, and Connor—well, anyone could see the boy had a burr under his saddle. His passive-aggressive attitude made it difficult to enjoy the meal. Even being offered his own car for college had done little to soften his hostility.

After dinner, Torus appeared in the entryway to the dining room, whining to be taken for a walk.

"All right, big fella. I hear you." Connor retrieved the dog's leash from the coat closet. "We'll be right back," he said to his mom.

When Connor stepped outside to take the dog for a walk, Reid breathed a sigh of relief and rose from his chair. "I'll help you clear the table."

Allison stood and began stacking dinner dishes. "No need. I've got this."

Reid muttered, "Seems like nobody wants my company this evening." He flexed his back again and glanced toward the sideboard.

Moving closer, he inspected the drawing he had been gifted. It really was a work of art.

Clearly, Connor had talent. He had captured the subtle nuances of the image, and his use of light and shadow was first rate.

He looked toward Allison. "What was all that business with this drawing? Why make such a big production out of offering a gift?"

"He wants you to be proud of him."

"I am."

"For the right reasons."

"What does that mean?"

Allison stepped forward to touch her husband's face. "You're exhausted. I can see it in the way you move. Go in and get comfortable. I'll bring you some coffee, and we can talk."

When Torus returned home without his master, Reid set out to find his son. Merely concerned at first, he became increasingly anxious as his search progressed. The flashlight's beam probed darkened recesses and swept expanses of open ground. It lit the black spaces under picnic tables and tracked the asphalt path.

With each passing minute, Reid's sense of dread worsened. Connor would never abandon Torus or leave him to run off on his own. He imagined his son lying somewhere, moaning in pain, having been pummeled by a mugger's fists. He even briefly considered the notion that Connor had been kidnapped and was being held for ransom. He struggled to put these and even more gruesome scenarios out of his mind.

"You're being irrational," he told himself. "The boy is seventeen years old. He's bright and capable of defending himself. There must be a logical explanation."

But then he saw the shape lying beside the path. At first, his mind refused to admit that the lifeless figure was a body. As he drew near, the truth became undeniable. A person or persons unknown had blown a hole through Connor's head, spilling his brains out onto the cold asphalt.

Reid turned aside and vomited. He wanted to cry, to scream, to lash out. His only son, the heir to his fortune, the child who was to carry on the family name was dead.

As the haze of numbness began to fade, the magnitude of what had been taken from him became apparent. The boy he loved, his only child, was gone. If he could have in his wrath, he would've torn the fabric of the universe asunder.

A spark of fury ignited a bonfire of hatred within Reid's soul. Tiny at first, the anger would grow until it had become a blazing rage. As he helplessly cradled his dead son's body, he vowed that the person who had committed this atrocity would pay. He would track down his son's killer even to the ends of the earth. He would find the man, and that man would then know the ferocity of a father's wrath. He would have his revenge.

5

DESPERATION

Early May 2016

Ruben Walker stepped out of the pawnshop with $23.72 in hand. The amount was less than he had hoped for but more than he should have received.

He had pawned a brass teapot, a hand-painted flowerpot, and an onyx brooch that had once belonged to his grandmother. It was the only keepsake his mother had treasured after being cast out by her father when she had become pregnant.

Deciding to pawn the brooch had been difficult for Ruben, but he had reasoned that when his mother returned, they could reclaim it—*if* she returned. The odds were growing slim; she had been gone for over a month.

Before exiting the pawnshop, Ruben looked back to acknowledge the clerk with a nod of appreciation. Clearly, the man had wanted to refuse the flowerpot but had taken it anyway, apparently moved by Ruben's obvious plight. The man waved back and wished Ruben good luck.

Out on the sidewalk, Ruben looked up. The sun rode high in the afternoon sky. He shaded his eyes to survey the neighborhood, noting every person within view.

Such had become his custom since his mother's disappearance. Eminently expecting her return, he assumed she would show up as abruptly as she had vanished. Not knowing the circumstance of her disappearance was perhaps worse than the trauma of a sixteen-year-old being left to fend for himself.

Ruben turned and began walking toward the mom-and-pop grocery store a block and a half away, his hands in the pockets of his threadbare jeans. He had a choice to make, though it wasn't much of a choice at all. He could apply the money in his pocket toward the rent that was due, or he could buy food for his siblings.

In the market, he added a half gallon of milk, a carton of eggs, a package of mac and cheese, plus a few other staples to his basket. As provisions go, it wasn't much, but the groceries would have to do. What troubled Ruben deeply was that they were running out of things to pawn.

The young man made his way home, carrying his paltry bag of edibles, his mind on the events surrounding his mother's disappearance.

The police had questioned everyone they could, including him, his siblings, and his mother's coworkers at both her places of employment. They had canvassed the neighborhood door-to-door and spoken with bus drivers and taxicab drivers alike. They had even tapped into their network of confidential informants.

No one had heard a thing. Initially, her fate had become a topic of speculation in the local media—both on television and in regional tabloids. Yet in recent days, interest in her disappearance had begun to wane.

The muscles at the angles of Ruben's jaw tightened. The bottom line was that his mother was gone, and she would either be found or she wouldn't. In either case, it was up to him to hold the family together.

When Ruben returned to the apartment, which was still being rented in his mother's name, Travis was on the floor, playing with the twins.

Travis, as second oldest, had been appointed babysitter-in-chief since the family could no longer afford day care for Felicia and Davon. As a result, Travis hadn't been to school in weeks, but then neither had Ruben.

After putting the groceries away, Ruben sat down on the divan and watched his two-year-old sister stack wooden blocks in a haphazard tower that easily toppled over.

What will she become? he wondered. *What path will her life follow? Will she get an education or be thrust into the world before she's ready? Will she marry well or be taken advantage of by serial lovers?* Whatever course lay before her, he resolved to be there to help her make the best choices.

Travis sat back from helping Davon build a maze out of crayons. He looked at his older brother. "Mr. Vinchenzo stopped by. I didn't open the door, but I could tell it was him by the sound of his voice. He says the rent is past due. I didn't know what to tell him."

"Don't worry about it," Ruben proclaimed with false bravado. "I'll take care of it."

"I don't like that guy," Travis said. "It's like he's pissed off all the time."

"That's just him. He's not really angry. It just seems that way."

"Yeah, well, he smells like garlic."

"Is that so?" Ruben asked. "And what do you smell like?"

Travis sniffed an armpit and then smiled at his older brother. "I smell like me."

"I'm hungry," Davon said as he positioned several crayons, creating a pattern only he could decipher.

"Me too," Ruben said gently, "but it's not time to eat yet."

Then Felicia chimed in. "Me too."

"I know. Tell you what—" Ruben rose from the divan to enter the kitchen area. Reaching into a cupboard, he brought down the package of Fig Newtons he had just purchased.

After carefully slicing open one end with a paring knife, he took out two cookies and carried them into the living room, where he presented one to each of the twins.

When Travis made a forlorn face, Ruben shrugged in a way that said, "Tough luck." He then changed his mind and returned to fetch a third cookie, which he handed to his younger brother. "That'll have to hold you guys till dinnertime. We can't eat everything all at once."

Standing near where his siblings were playing, Ruben looked down at Travis and said, "Are you guys okay for a while? I need to talk to our landlord."

Travis responded with a thumbs-up. "Sure. I'm cool."

"Good. But remember that if I find more than three cookies missing when I get back, you're gonna be sorry."

"Don't worry. They're safe."

"Right. I'll be back soon." Ruben descended the stairs to the first floor.

En route, he rehearsed the excuses he planned to give. As he turned various phrases over it in his mind, they sounded more like pleading and begging than solving the matter of the delinquent rent.

Salvador Vinchenzo answered promptly when Ruben knocked on his door. He was a swarthy man with a potbelly and a healthy growth of black stubble on his cheeks and jowls. He wore a white T-shirt and khaki trousers.

"Ah, Ruben," the landlord said, "you finally decided to come see me, eh?" Salvador raked a handful of pudgy fingers through his balding hair.

"I'm sorry, Mr. Vinchenzo. I know we're late, but it's been hard."

"I get that—your mother missing and all. Has there been any word?"

Ruben shook his head.

"Why would a woman do that—up and leave her kids?"

"It's not her fault," Ruben declared vehemently. "When she comes back, she'll tell you."

"Easy there. I meant no disrespect. Okay?"

Ruben nodded. "About the rent—"

"I know. I know. Look, I wouldn't press except I can't afford to lose my job. You see, I don't own this building. I only work for the guy who does, and he's been on my case. Do you have any money—any at all?"

"I did, but I spent it on food."

"That's a shame—I mean—the owner's got me in a bad place. I need to show I can manage things here, or I'll be the one looking for a new place to live. Can't you afford to pay something, anything?"

"Not yet, but if you give me two weeks, I'm sure I can get some cash together. This morning, I thought I had a job lined up, but—"

"It's tough finding work when you're young. How old are you if I might ask?"

"I'm eighteen."

Salvador cocked his head and scowled in obvious disbelief.

"Sixteen," Ruben admitted reluctantly.

The landlord shook his head.

"No. It's true. I had a birthday last month, and I'm a good worker."

"Maybe so, but here's the way things stand. I'm sorry your mom ain't around no more, but we don't run a charity here. I'll give you two weeks. That's the best I can do. If you don't have the rent by then, you'll have to move out. I don't have a choice, okay? No hard feelings."

"Nah, you're just doing your job."

"It's good you understand."

As Ruben turned away, his spirits began to lift. Two weeks was a long time. Who knew? Anything could happen.

Encouraged by having gained an extension on the rent, Ruben decided to treat his family to a special surprise. He fished in his pocket to see how much money was left. He pulled out $1.87. It would be enough.

Rather than return to the apartment, he headed back to the market. The twins especially would appreciate an unexpected indulgence.

At the market, Ruben purchased a large candy bar stuffed with caramel and nuts. When divided four ways, the portions would seem meager, but it was the gesture, not the size of the treat, that was important.

Candy bar in hand, Ruben returned home. To his surprise, a late-model car he didn't recognize was parked in front of his apartment building. Parked beside it was a police cruiser.

As he climbed the stairs to the second floor, Ruben sensed that something was amiss. The sound of the twins at play usually spilled out into the corridor, but as he approached the apartment, all was quiet.

Upon entering the apartment, it wasn't his siblings that Ruben first encountered. Instead, a middle-aged woman with wire-rimmed glasses and a cop in uniform were standing in the middle of the floor as if waiting for him to return. The woman had on beige slacks and a pale yellow blouse. She wore her red hair swept into a tight bun at the back of her head. She held a leather portfolio hooked under one arm.

The cop stood loosely at attention, his arms at his sides. His black belt and black shoes gleamed with a dark luster. A holstered 9 mm semiautomatic pistol rested menacingly on his hip.

Ruben's gaze darted around the apartment. Except for the two strangers, the place was empty.

"Ruben," said the woman, "don't be alarmed. I'm Ms. Bartholomew from Child Protective Services. We're here to help."

"How do you know who I am?"

Ms. Bartholomew tapped the portfolio. "We opened a case file on your family when your mother disappeared. I'm sorry it's taken us so long to come for you, but in recent months, our department has been appallingly understaffed, budget cuts being what they are."

"Where are my brothers and my sister!" Ruben exclaimed.

"They're safe." Ms. Bartholomew indicated the divan. "Let's sit down. We can talk."

Ruben balled his fists, forgetting the candy bar he was carrying. "Tell me where they are. What have you done with them?"

The cop tensed ever so slightly.

"Please," Ms. Bartholomew said soothingly. "I'm sure you have many questions. Come sit with me, and I'll explain everything."

Ruben stood motionless for a time, deciding what to do. Who was this woman? And why was a cop planted like a tree in the middle of their apartment, acting as if he owned the place? What was going on?

"Please?" Ms. Bartholomew crossed over to the divan and sat down. She patted the cushion beside her.

Ruben reluctantly moved to join her but seated himself an arm's length away.

Ms. Bartholomew smoothed her slacks at her knees. "I'm a caseworker with Child Protective Services. CPS is a state agency charged with safeguarding the welfare of children. We look after kids who've been abused or abandoned—"

"We're not abandoned. My mother will come back. You'll see."

"I'm sure she will, but in the meantime, you guys are on your own. It's the agency's job to make sure you are properly cared for."

"No," Ruben retorted. "It's my job. Travis and the twins are my responsibility."

"I can appreciate how you feel." Ms. Bartholomew reached out to touch Ruben's shoulder. He pulled away. Unfazed, the caseworker continued, "It's good when siblings look out for one another, and I'm sure you do your best. Unfortunately, the law doesn't regard you as being an adult. In the eyes of the state, you're simply not qualified to be your siblings' guardian."

"They're my family," Ruben snapped. "I'm the oldest. That makes them my responsibility. I don't care what the state says."

Ms. Bartholomew frowned. "I didn't come here to argue with you."

"Why did you come?"

The caseworker paused a moment as if letting the tension in the room ease. Calmly she said, "All you children are to be placed in foster homes, where you'll be well-cared for. Most importantly, you'll be safe and well-fed. You have no idea the kinds of evils children on their own can encounter—the things I've seen."

She sighed deeply and shook her head.

"Ruben, I appreciate your loyalty to your siblings, but you're just not ready to be their guardian. I mean, look around. There's hardly a stick of furniture left in this apartment. You've had to pawn what little there was, haven't you? Also, I understand that you and your brother haven't been to school in quite a while. How do you think you and he will fare in this world without an education?"

Ruben flushed. "I'm going to get a job. I'm a good worker."

"What if you can't? Not many sixteen-year-olds can find employment that pays well enough to support a family. You don't want your brothers and sisters to go without, do you? Think of their welfare. You know they'll be better off in a stable environment with people who are qualified to look after them."

"Where did you take them?" Ruben demanded.

Ms. Bartholomew squared her shoulders. "I think it's best if we don't share that information right now. Perhaps later when you've had a chance to process the situation appropriately. Otherwise, you might feel inclined to take matters into your own hands. Just believe me when I tell you that they're safe and properly looked after."

"What about me? Are you going to take me to jail too?"

"It's not jail, Ruben. Foster homes are nothing like that. Usually there are other children in the home like a real family."

"We are a real family, and you want to split us up."

"Kids living on their own without parents around isn't a real family." Ms. Bartholomew stood up. "We can talk more about this after you're settled in." She glanced at her watch. "I have other clients to visit. This gentleman will take you to begin your processing. Please don't resist. It won't accomplish a thing. It will only make matters worse. You need to trust me in this. I've been down this road many times."

The cop stepped forward. Ruben readied himself to fight back. But then the cop halted, as if inviting Ruben to make a decision.

Briefly the boy toyed with the idea of fleeing, but the cop looked to be in decent shape and capable of catching him. Besides, attempting to escape would be foolish unless he was convinced he could get away. It seemed he was trapped. He let himself be escorted downstairs.

On the sidewalk, Ruben glanced up at the second-story window.

One day, he promised himself, *we will be a family again. They can't keep me locked up forever. Somehow I'll find Travis and the twins, and we'll be together again. This I swear.*

The cop settled him in the squad car and closed the door.

Ten months later, on March 21, 2017, Ruben woke up in a broken freezer. He had chanced upon the discarded appliance behind an abandoned house while roaming lower-class neighborhoods the preceding night. Tipped on its side and with its lid propped up as an awning of sorts, it had offered decent shelter. At least it had partially shielded him from the cold late-winter winds.

Before climbing in, he had tested the freezer's latch, making certain it was smashed thoroughly enough that he wouldn't be trapped inside.

After wrapping discarded newspapers around his feet and legs, he had slept fitfully. The backpack that contained the sum of his worldly goods had served as a lumpy pillow.

A week had elapsed since he had run away from his fourth foster home, and the strain of again living on the streets was taking its toll.

Feeling tired and hungry, even thinking about the long day ahead filled him with dread. Ruben crawled out to face the gathering dawn. His fingers and toes were cold and numb.

After retrieving his backpack, he shoved a hand into his pants pocket, confirming that all the money he had in the world was still there.

By hustling odd jobs and doing day labor, he had managed to scrape together a little over one hundred dollars. It wasn't much, but it was a start. In a couple months, if he continued his miserly ways, he might have enough to rent an apartment and begin the process of putting his family back together.

During the first couple days, he had found employment by searching online websites that listed odd jobs that needed doing. He had accessed the websites using the cell phone his foster parents had given him.

But then his cell service had been abruptly discontinued. He figured the foster couple had dropped him from their plan, which probably was a good thing. It was too tempting to rely upon a cell phone for the services it provided. Eventually, the cops were sure to run a trace and track him down. He had sold the phone for twenty bucks.

After studying his surroundings to make sure nobody was monitoring his activities, Ruben headed out to begin his day. He would start with construction sites he had mentally noted during his previous sojourns. With luck, a craftsman might need a step-and-fetch-it or a cleanup man. Who knew, perhaps he could land a position that would become more than a day job.

Twenty minutes later, as he passed an alley in a rough neighborhood, he suddenly felt a hard object pressed roughly against his ribs. A gruff voice whispered in his ear, "You make a sound, and I'll blow you away. Now give me your money—all of it, and be quick about it."

Ruben started to turn his head to see who was robbing him, but a second sharp pain stopped him.

"Try that again, and you're dead," said the voice. "You carrying heat?"

"No."

"What's in the knapsack?"

"Clothes, a toothbrush, a tin cup—nothing of value to you."

"Hand it over."

Ruben bridled his anger and reluctantly did as instructed. He heard the backpack being zipped open, and sounds that indicated the thief was rummaging through his paltry possessions. Then the backpack was cast aside.

"See, I told you," Ruben said.

A gush of hot breath blew past Ruben's ear. "Dude, this is how it works. You give me money, or I kill you where you stand. You feel me? Now hand over what you got." Another stab of pain declared that the thief was serious.

Having been robbed before, Ruben knew the drill. Comply and maybe all you lose is your money. Fight back and things get ugly, perhaps even lethal. Even knowing the risks, he hesitated. The cash in his pocket was his entire worldly fortune.

A new pain flared at the base of Ruben's skull. A cold hard object was being thrust against the back of his neck. "Last chance, dude. Pay or die. I ain't fooling with you."

Years before, Ruben had watched a movie where a victim had disarmed an assailant by spinning around suddenly and wrestling the gun from his hand. He had thought at the time that the scenario was ludicrous.

How long, he had wondered, *does it take for a determined mugger to squeeze a trigger—a fraction of a second?*

With a grunt of resignation, he fished in his pocket and pulled out his cash. "It's all I got."

"Not anymore." The pressure eased. "Now start walking, and don't look back."

"Are you going to shoot me?"

"I guess you're about to find out."

"Can I get my backpack?"

"Why not? Just don't turn around."

As Ruben bent down to retrieve his backpack, he kept his eyes fixed on the pavement ahead. He slung the backpack over his shoulder.

"Now start walking," said the voice, which sounded far away, as if his assailant was already retreating into the alley.

At a slow pace, Ruben walked forward, expecting at any minute to feel the crunch of a bullet ripping into his spine. A block later, he looked back. The street was empty.

Toward the middle of the afternoon after having been robbed, Ruben found himself in his old neighborhood. He had previously resolved to stay away for fear of being recognized and reported, but something had drawn him—perhaps a need to be near the only home he had known.

A sullen bitterness had settled in—a smoldering anger that chased away reason and clouded his judgment. All he could think about was his shattered dreams. The hope he had nurtured for reuniting his family had been severely eroded, leaving him feeling impotent and vulnerable. More than ever, he realized he was desperately alone.

While aimlessly walking streets that all seemed the same and passing rows of small shops that failed to attract his notice, he tried to envision what to do next, but his thoughts were too jumbled. Then out of the corner of his eye, he noticed a flower shop's cargo van double-parked at the curb. Its sliding side door was open, and its engine was running, but the driver was nowhere to be seen. Ruben figured the fellow was probably delivering a floral arrangement inside one of the nearby apartment buildings.

On impulse, Ruben jumped into the van and began rummaging under the seats and in the crevices where things sometimes fall, searching for anything worth stealing. That he would intentionally commit a theft was testimony to his state of mind.

The lessons his mother had planted in his heart were deeply rooted; he had promised himself never to take anything that didn't belong to him. But then if others could profit from stealing, why shouldn't he?

Ruben discovered a quarter forgotten under a floor mat but nothing else of worth, not even when he rummaged through the center console. But when he opened the glove box, he encountered a surprise.

A jet-black .40-caliber pistol lay beneath a jumble of papers. Without thinking, he snatched the pistol and stuffed it into the waistband of his trousers, pulling his shirt down to conceal it. Then he snapped the glove box shut and hastily returned to the sidewalk. Acting as if nothing had transpired, he continued on his way, alert for sounds of pursuit. There were none.

A strange sensation began to envelop Ruben—a sense of empowerment and a burgeoning confidence that he was about to become the master of his own destiny. He longed to retrieve the pistol from his waistband and feel its weight in his hands. He had never handled a gun before, but he had witnessed enough entertainment media to know how they worked. He wanted to test the action of the slide and cock the hammer. He wanted to pull the trigger. Instead, he walked on.

Rather than continue turning down streets at random, Ruben headed in a westerly direction; his imagination focused on how his fortunes were about to change. No longer would he be the victim. No longer would he be subjected to the will of others. He now possessed a means to defend himself.

Slowly it dawned upon him that he was now able to shape his own destiny. He could do unto others as they had done unto him.

Three miles farther on, Ruben found himself in Menlo Park. It was the first time he had ever visited that community despite having lived so near.

As night fell, he entered Drystone Park and began trekking its asphalt paths. A desperate scheme had formed in the back of his mind. The weapon now in his possession would allow him to find some rich dude and take his money. He would strike back against the misfortunes that had plagued his life. No longer would he be the helpless prey of circumstance. Now he was the master.

A crescent moon hung high overhead. Leaves fluttered in the gentle breeze. A few stars dotted the night sky.

Ruben looked ahead and saw a figure approaching on the path. The young man seemed near his own age, perhaps a little older. He was well-dressed in a thin windbreaker, denim jeans, and designer sneakers that must have cost a small fortune. The night was too dark to make out the features of the young man's face.

Surely this guy must have a wad of cash on him, Ruben thought. Then he noted a dog bounding across the grass, trailing his leash; it was obviously not a guard dog since he was running free.

Ruben pulled the pistol from his waistband and cocked it. He then held it low, keeping it out of sight behind his hip. A sudden realization came to him that what he was about to do was wrong, but he cast the thought aside. All he knew was that he was desperate; he had come to the end of himself.

When the dude drew near, Ruben stepped directly in front of him and raised the pistol. "Give me your money," he demanded. The darkness prevented him from seeing the surprise in the young man's eyes.

Startled, his intended victim stopped dead in his tracks and then laughed. "Come on. Who do you think you are, Jesse James?"

"Who?" Ruben said in confusion.

"The famous road agent—never mind. Look, I don't have any money to give you. I'm just out walking my dog."

Ruben's hand shook as he thrust the pistol toward his target. "Man, this is how it works. Give me money, or I'll shoot you."

"I told you, I don't have any money. I left my wallet at home."

"I don't believe you. All you rich guys are the same. You always have money."

The young man took one step forward. He held his hands out, palms up. "Not this time. I don't even have cab fare."

"Look, man, I'm not kidding. Pay me or die."

"Fine, if that's the way it is"—the dude took another step forward—"you can have whatever I've got." He began to slowly reach for his back pocket but then in a flash reversed directions and lunged forward to knock the gun away. Instead, he missed and grazed the sleeve of Ruben's shirt.

Reflexively Ruben jerked his gun hand back. In so doing, he accidentally pulled the trigger. The bullet struck the young man in the forehead. As if in slow motion, his victim crumpled to the ground and did not move.

Stunned and with the sound of the gunshot reverberating in his ears, Ruben stood motionless while he fought to comprehend what had just transpired. Then like a sleepwalker startled to wakefulness, he numbly looked around in confusion. The park appeared to be empty except for the dog now bounding in his direction. He turned and ran. The dog did not pursue.

Ruben ran and ran, his heart pounding and his pulse thudding in his ears. When he felt he was far enough away, he used his shirttail to wipe the gun clean and then ditched the weapon down a storm drain. Continuing, he walk-jogged as fast as he could without attracting undue notice. In time, he made his way back to East Palo Alto.

A new set of emotions settled in, far more terrible than any he had previously known. He felt a crushing sense of guilt merged with an abject dread of being identified as a killer.

Somehow he made his way back to the abandoned house and the busted freezer. As he huddled inside with the door lowered, all he could think was that he was now a wanted criminal, a murderer. What would his siblings say? What would his mother think when she returned?

In the darkness, he curled up in a fetal position, shivering not from cold but from the terror that gripped his soul.

6

TRANSITIONS

Early April 2017

Two weeks after Connor's murder, Reid sat in his office at ERA Inc. Like some scene from a science fiction movie, surreal images flickered across the face of his flat-panel monitor. For over an hour, he had been staring at the design team's latest product, an experiential rendering that his staff was calling synthetic reality. The app's vivid graphics and informational content were amazing, but Reid was finding it virtually impossible to keep his mind on his work.

With a start, he realized that his attention had drifted again. Connor's childhood had come to mind and his excitement after moving into the Silver Vale House. Reid visualized how the two-year-old had scampered about marking interesting places to play. He also pictured the house in recent days—the abiding silence, the forlorn emptiness, and how his home had seemed to grow so much larger.

Reid switched off his workstation and stood up, troubled by the realization that he was doing nothing more than wasting time. He clenched his jaw, feeling that perhaps he should set about doing something that truly mattered.

That morning, he had again phoned the detective in charge to request his daily update. Though they had been sympathetic at first after two weeks of repeated interruptions, the authorities were growing annoyed. One officer had come straight out and said, "We're the professionals here, so stop interfering. Let us do our job. We will let you know if anything changes."

Frustrated and annoyed, Reid had refrained from reminding them it was his son who had died, not theirs. Only a fool antagonizes people who are trying to help. Still, he had no intention of being sidelined during the continuing investigation.

Reid reached into the top drawer of his desk and took out the Colt model 1911 that he had purchased from a firearms dealer the week before. The salesman had assured him that the .45 caliber semiautomatic was absolutely the best handgun for personal defense.

Being unfamiliar with weapons, Reid had taken the man at his word. The problem was that the pistol felt bulky as he slipped it awkwardly into the concealed holster clipped to his belt. He then drew on the extra-large hoodie he had purchased at a thrift store. The sweatshirt was bulky enough to hide the weapon's bulge.

Before leaving his office, Reid looked back at his desk and the documents and folders that still demanded his attention. Work was piling up. A month earlier, he would've felt an overriding compulsion to deal with every problem. Now he didn't care. A new reality had overtaken his life. He stepped into the corridor and headed toward the main exit.

During the first week after Connor's murder, Reid had canvassed the neighborhood in a five-block radius centered at the crime scene. He had posted a reward of ten thousand dollars payable to anyone willing to come forward with information.

Several days later, he had increased the reward to fifteen thousand and then twenty thousand. After the police had finished with Drystone Park, he had conducted his own investigation, meticulously inspecting every square inch, searching for clues without success. Then he had begun canvassing the streets, questioning people at random, hoping to find a witness. No one would admit to having seen or heard a thing. Now it was time to go hunting.

"If anyone asks," Reid instructed Melissa, the receptionist at the front desk, "I'll be away for the afternoon. They can leave a message."

"Very well, Mr. Scott." The young woman attempted to hide her disapproval; it seemed as if she found it reprehensible that her employer would take off in the middle of the day without an explanation.

"Hold up," Gavin Marsh called ahead as he hurried to catch up before his boss could exit the front door. Drawing near, he took hold of Reid's upper arm. "Where do you think you're going?" He seemed out of breath.

"You need to get more exercise," Reid commented tersely as he looked around, noting that the front lobby was otherwise deserted.

"Tell me about it. Which reminds me, scuttlebutt is you joined a gym."

"I felt the need to get in shape. Is that a problem?"

"It's just that working out has never been your thing."

"It takes my mind off—What do you want?"

"Oh." Gavin let go of Reid's arm. "Just making sure you remember we have a staff meeting at one fifteen."

"I do, but I won't be there."

"Boss, we need your input. It's time to pick the rendering methodology we're going to use going forward. The programmers can't do anything more until we make our selection."

"Charlie knows the pros and cons of what's available. Listen to what he has to say and then go with his recommendation. We'll be fine."

"Are you feeling well? You're not talking like the Reid Scott I used to know. That guy would never have delegated such a major responsibility."

"Maybe it's time for me to step away for a while. Maybe it's past time. If I'd let go sooner—"

"Are you suggesting what I think you are? You realize, I hope, that what happened to Connor is not your fault. God has a destiny for each of us. Nothing you could have done would've changed how things turned out."

"You're saying God killed my son?"

"No. Certainly not. God endowed mankind with free will. He lets us do what we do for good or evil. But when tragedy overtakes us, like losing a son, God can turn adversity into something good no matter what the circumstances."

With great incredulity, Reid declared, "You're telling me God regards my son's murder as something good?"

"Not at all. Connor's murder was an act of pure evil, plain and simple. Please understand. What I'm saying is that God can make it so that even the worst evil has a good outcome. I've seen it happen, like when my sister was diagnosed with cancer. All that's needed is for us to believe."

"Gavin, sometimes I truly wish I shared your faith, but I don't. Look, I've gotta go. Like I said, listen to Charlie. Go with whatever he thinks is best." Reid hurried out the front door, leaving Gavin to swallow the retort balanced on the tip of his tongue.

The next day while seated in an internet café, Reid was doing his best to look inconspicuous. When he sipped his caramel latte, it tasted far too sweet. He set the drink aside.

For more than two hours, a steady stream of customers had filtered in and out through the front door. He had ignored the foot traffic and instead had hunched over his laptop, scanning online news articles, visiting chat rooms, and reviewing crime statistics. The muscles in his back ached. He flexed to relieve the discomfort.

A simple question had prompted Reid's review of the news archives. "What areas in Silicon Valley," he had asked himself, "have the highest crime rates?" The question had stood a corollary to Sutton's law.

Willie Sutton, a bank robber, had once been asked, "Why do you rob banks?" Sutton had replied, "Because that's where the money is."

While considering his son's murder, a string of ideas had occurred to Reid. First off, Connor was universally well-liked and had virtually no enemies. Therefore, the most likely motive for the crime must have been a robbery gone awry.

And since Menlo Park and the surrounding communities were highly affluent, most likely the perpetrator had ventured in from somewhere else. Keeping these deductions in mind, Reid had recalled Sutton's law: "Go where the money is."

In fact, patterns had emerged during his archival analysis. Of special interest were the reports of increased gang activity in East Palo Alto. Shifting his investigation away from Menlo Park would be a long shot, but as he glanced around the bistro, he decided to start his reconnaissance there because if seemed the right thing to do.

"Yep, the best way to catch fish is to fish where fish like to swim," Reid whispered to himself as he switched off his laptop and returned it to its travel case. The unfinished portion of his latte went into the trash bin.

Out on the street again, he turned toward where he had parked half a block away. As he approached his Lexus, a sudden realization struck him: He would need a much less pretentious car. Cruising through impoverished neighborhoods in a fancy sedan would invite trouble. He could also do with a new set of clothes—something more working-class, more plebeian. He hauled out his cell phone and searched online for the nearest thrift store.

The stink of rotting garbage and human excrement filled the air. Trash cluttered the ground and clung to the branches of low-lying shrubs where the wind had blown it.

Three weeks after Connor's death, Reid carefully navigated his way through the homeless camp, mindful not to intrude on sites where somebody had already staked a claim.

Only moments before, he had wandered too close to a vagrant's hovel. His intrusion had drawn an angry tirade and threats of violence. Rather than pick a fight, he had apologized and hurried on.

The Colt 45 strapped to Reid's belt pressed hard against his flank. He felt the weight of it at his hip. Every day during the preceding week, he had spent at least an hour practicing at home, repeatedly drawing his weapon and dry firing at imaginary targets. Twice, he had visited a shooting range to engage in live fire training.

With his elbow, Reid shifted the pistol to ease the pressure. From a sheltered corner of his mind, a half-formed thought emerged to trouble him: What did it signify that he was becoming comfortable with an object so lethal? He tugged the tail of his extra-large hoodie down, making certain the pistol was properly concealed.

The homeless camp he had chosen to visit lay on the outskirts of East Palo Alto. Reid had asked around, hinting that he needed a place to sleep where the police would leave him in peace.

This camp was the one most often recommended. Like an oasis in an urban desert, a copse of cottonwoods sheltered one side of the refuge. A seasonal stream ran along another.

Being relatively isolated, the site was generally known as a haven for drug activity and other types of criminal behavior, which suited his purposes well.

Remembering the adage that it takes a thief to catch a thief, Reid had formulated a plan. If he could entice someone to rob him, he would apprehend the scoundrel and then interrogate him about other criminal activities. Maybe in such a fashion, he could repetitively work his way up the chain of bad guys until he had identified Connor's killer. Admittedly, his plan was pathetic, but lacking other options, it was the best he could come up with, and there was a slight possibility it just might work.

Slung over one shoulder, Reid carried a burlap sack that contained a lumpy sleeping bag, a canvas tarp, a dented pot, a plastic water bottle, and other odds and ends. The bag made a clinking sound as he walked. He hoped it would attract attention. The more people who witnessed his arrival, the more likely he'd be marked as a newbie and therefore an easy target.

The idea of using himself as bait had come to him one night while lying in bed at home, unable to sleep. The notion had seemed perfectly reasonable at the time. Now he wasn't so sure, but then he had reminded himself: Nothing ventured; nothing gained. You need cheese to catch a mouse, and he was the cheese.

Moving on, Reid came to a vacant spot at the periphery of the camp. The rocky ground sloped a bit, and his sleeping area would be cramped, but it would do. After unrolling his sleeping bag, he strung his tarp as a makeshift lean-to. He then set out the possessions he had brought along, making it seem as if he intended to stay.

When dusk turned to night, Reid lay down fully clothed in his sleeping bag, leaving the edges unzipped. With care he positioned the .45 under the burlap bag, which he used as a pillow. He closed his eyes and pretended to be asleep. He did not have to wait long.

A rustling sound, barely audible, came to him above the background hum of the surrounding city. He tensed his muscles but kept his breathing steady as he listened with his eyes closed. A twig snapped. The noise stopped, and there was nothing.

Reid waited. He longed to open his eyes and study his surroundings. Instead, he strained to hear even the faintest noise.

Perhaps it had only been his imagination. He remembered reading once that if you expect trouble, you're likely to find it even where none existed before.

Then there came the scrape of a foot against the rocky ground. Whoever was moving toward him was being extremely deliberate. With equal care, he slowly slid his hand under the burlap bag until his fingers gripped the pistol.

The pungent reek of an unwashed body reached Reid's nostrils. He involuntarily flinched. The intruder startled and drew his hand back, having already latched onto the handle of the dented pot.

With one hand, Reid yanked the pistol out from beneath the burlap bag. With the other, he threw off the sleeping bag and sat bolt upright. In one swift motion, he pointed the muzzle of the Colt directly at the would-be thief, just as he had practiced at home. And just as he had practiced at home, he instinctively squeezed the trigger, but nothing happened. He had forgotten to release the safety.

Illuminated by the light of a three-quarter moon, Reid found himself staring into the terrified face of a man who had to be more than seventy years old. His scraggly gray beard bore the stains of tobacco juice. His skin was as brown and as rough as old shoe leather. His bloodshot eyes had gone wide with fright. Clearly, the emaciated fellow was no murderer.

The man stammered, "I'm sorry, mister. I ain't meant no harm. Here, take it back—" He held the pot out in his shaking hands.

A crushing sense of dismay swept over Reid. He had nearly shot the man. He had come perilously close to taking the life of a vagrant, whose only crime was pilfering a worthless pot. "Drop it and get the hell out of here," he cursed in a husky voice.

"Yes, sir. I surely will. Don't you shoot me now." The man cautiously deposited the pot on the ground and hastily backed away with his hands held high in the air.

As Reid lowered the pistol, he noted that his own hands had begun to shake. When the man was far away, he set about to unload the weapon, but the shaking had become too intense. So instead, he stuffed the Colt into his burlap bag.

What am I doing here? he wondered. *How did I get from losing Connor to this moment?*

He tried to connect the dots, but his only thought was that he had come perilously close to committing the same sin that had befallen his son.

A nauseating gush of bile rose in the back of Reid's throat. Overcome with self-loathing, he hurriedly gathered up his few belongings and, by the moon's feeble light, stumbled back to where he had parked his rented Toyota coupe three blocks away.

Reid sat cross-legged on a downtown sidewalk in East Palo Alto; his back pressed against the brick wall of a secondhand store.

It was early evening, and the store had just closed. Less than forty-eight hours had passed since his confrontation at the homeless camp. The memory of having nearly killed a man still haunted him.

Time and again, he had tried to chase the incident from his mind, but the terrified look in the old man's eyes seemed to have been permanently seared into his consciousness. That he would return to the streets to resume his search spoke volumes. Such was the power of the compulsion that enthralled him.

What frightened Reid most was the understanding that morally he was no better than the man who had killed his son. His all-consuming hatred had pushed him to the brink of taking another man's life. Only his unfamiliarity with firearms had saved him from committing the act. From an ethical standpoint, he was as guilty as any other murderer and just as worthy of shame and condemnation.

Across the street, a steady flow of vagrants entered the Bedrock Rescue Mission. The denizens of the street were gathering for an evening meal. Most wore what Reid had come to regard as urban camouflage: a heavy coat or a surplus army jacket, threadbare jeans, secondhand sneakers, and either a woolen skullcap or a baseball hat.

The Colt pistol no longer dug into Reid's flank. He had buried it deep in a dumpster, making certain it would never be found. The memory of it pressing against his hip caused his self-loathing to flare up again.

A man standing in front of the mission waved. Reid waved back. He knew the guy only by his street name, Sketch.

They had spoken several times, mostly about nothing special. The fellow had seemed affable enough if a little scattered in his thinking.

Rather than turn and enter the mission, Sketch hesitated. Peering at Reid, he cocked his head as if considering what to do. He then crossed the street to where Reid sat.

"How's it going?" Sketch said, drawing near.

"Not bad. You?" Reid replied, sensing what was to follow.

"Why ya sitting here?" Sketch said, looking down. He was a large man with broad shoulders and a thick chest.

"Just taking it all in."

"Any leads on who killed your son?"

"Not a one."

"That's a damn shame. I hope they catch the bum. Say, ain't you hungry?"

"Now that you mention it, I suppose I am."

Sketch wiped his nose on his sleeve and then gestured toward the mission. "You ever been to the Bedrock?"

Reid shook his head.

"It's a good place to score a meal. Come with me. I'll introduce you to Kyle. Kyle Long runs things. They make us sing for our dinner, but that's okay. And they pray a lot, but if you're hungry—"

Reid's stomach roiled at the thought of dining at a homeless shelter. "You go ahead. I'm fine here."

"Nonsense." Sketch reached down and literally hauled Reid to his feet. "Second rule of living homeless: Never turn down free food." The man was as strong as he appeared. Keeping a tight grip on Reid's arm, he steered him across the street. "You'll like Kyle. He's not a Holy Roller like some of them other dudes."

Upon being propelled through the mission's front door, Reid noted that there were more than seventy men crowded into the main hall. Nearly all had taken seats at folding tables arranged in orderly rows.

Muted conversations drifted up throughout the room. Reid found it easy to distinguish staff from clientele; staff members wore white aprons. A pair of long tables set end to end paralleled the far wall. A line of stainless steel serving pans stretched down the center of both tables. Lids covered most pans. Steam rose from the few that had been left uncovered.

Reid sniffed the air, which was surprisingly less pungent than expected, the room being populated by vagrants.

Keeping a tight grip on Reid's arm, Sketch steered him toward the men's restroom at the back of the hall. "House rules," he whispered. "Gotta wash up first—face and hands. There's a shower for them that truly needs it, but you gotta get here early. Not that I'm implying anything. You seem pretty spiffy for a guy in our situation."

When the two men returned to the hall after washing up, Reid noted that only a few chairs were still vacant, and no two empty chairs were side by side. He wondered if Sketch might suggest to one of his buddies that they relocate to make room.

But apparently, that wasn't the way things were done. His benefactor thrust his chin toward a chair at the back of the room. In a low voice, he instructed, "You sit there. Do what everybody else does. When we set to eating, I'll bring Kyle around to introduce you." Sketch then sauntered off to join two guys who greeted him with nods of recognition.

As Reid sat down, the other men at his table eyed him with suspicion but said nothing. He studied their faces. Not one seemed familiar.

Likewise, as he scanned the room, he identified only two fellows he had encountered during his reconnaissance missions.

Where have all these others been hiding? he wondered.

It seemed that what they claimed was true: The homeless do become invisible when it suits them. Then he did a double take, having assumed that only males had been invited to the gathering.

Seated in one corner, a group of women were numbered among the destitute. Apparently, poverty was impartial when it came to gender.

Looking around, Reid noted that only salt and pepper shakers, plus a squeeze bottle of ketchup, had been set out on every table. There were no individual place settings in view, though a clean plastic cloth graced every table.

A young woman advanced cheerily to the front of the room. She wore a simple lime-green dress that trailed to the middle of her calves. No whistles or catcalls rang out. All conversation fell silent.

As if on cue, the assemblage stood in unison. Reid followed suit. Someone switched on a portable CD player, and the gathering began singing "Rock of Ages" followed by "The Old Rugged Cross."

As the music progressed, the singing became more enthusiastic. No hymnals had been provided, so Reid was forced to conclude that the majority of those in attendance had memorized the words over a series of visits. It made him wonder how long some of his fellow street denizens had been gathering at the Bedrock.

When the worship period ended, the audience was invited to take their seats again. A small man with thinning hair stepped forward to recite a list of announcements. Questions were asked and answered. Then another speaker gave a brief but impassioned sermon—an upbeat message stressing hope and redemption.

Reid glanced around. Only here and there were members of the audience paying attention. The rest looked as if they had heard it all before.

When the business at hand concluded, the assemblage rose in unison and began shuffling toward the serving tables in orderly fashion. There was no pushing or shoving.

Reid gathered up a dinner plate, a fork, a knife, a spoon, and a paper napkin from racks at the head of the serving tables.

Single file, destitute men eased down the line, pointing to this or that. Volunteers on the opposite side of the table ladled servings onto their plates, receiving whispered thank-yous in return.

Reid assumed that the universal rule of etiquette applied: Take as much as you want, but eat as much as you take. Conversations were kept to a minimum until everyone had been served. Then a jumble of noise erupted throughout the hall.

Upon returning to his seat, Reid sampled his beef stew. It tasted surprisingly good. Even more remarkable, the carrots were crisp and the boiled potatoes not too mushy. The bread appeared to have been baked on site. He began to speculate on how many volunteers would have been needed to prepare the meal. He was still absorbed in his musings when

Sketch and another man stepped up behind him. Reid glanced up in response to a tap on his shoulder.

"This is Kyle Long," Sketch said. "He's our executive director. If you need anything, this is the guy to see."

Kyle extended his hand. "And your name is?"

Reid hastily rose from his chair and returned the handshake. "Reid. Reid S—"

"First names only please," Kyle said, cutting him off. "Our clients are more comfortable that way." His grip conveyed a sense of genuine hospitality.

The fellow seated just to Reid's right looked up. The expression on his face puzzled Reid until he realized he had responded with his real name rather than using a street alias. He thought about rectifying the oversight but couldn't bring a suitable nickname to mind.

"You're new to our community?" Kyle observed.

"Yeah. I've been on the streets now about a week and a half."

When the heads of two other men jerked up, Reid understood that he had committed a second gaffe by claiming he'd been homeless for such a short length of time.

Generally, homelessness was a state of being, not an event. Then the question's original intent came to him, and he stammered, "Oh. You mean is this my first visit? Yes, it is." He flushed as he scolded himself. *Idiot, talk about fitting right in—*

"Well, welcome friend." Kyle smiled warmly. "We're glad you decided to join us."

Reid looked at Sketch, who turned his face away to avoid making eye contact.

Reid studied the executive director. Something in Kyle's demeanor suggested a high level of compassion and a sense of self-assurance, as if the fellow felt completely comfortable in his own identity.

Standing tall, the executive director was a stout man with excellent posture and a flat abdomen. Yet there was nothing threatening about him. He wore his full head of dark hair neatly trimmed and precisely parted on one side. There was a hint of mirth in his azure eyes, and there was something more.

Reid took a second look. *What am I seeing here?* he wondered. *Intelligence? Wisdom beyond his years?* Perception. That's what he was sensing. Suddenly he had the clear impression his soul was being measured.

"After dinner," Kyle suggested casually, "if you're not too pressed for time, I'd like to meet with you. Think we could visit for a bit? Just to talk? If you'd rather not, I understand. It's just that I like to get to know those who share a meal with us. What do you say?"

A feeling of uneasiness welled up inside Reid. Refusing after having been treated to a free dinner would seem rude. Accepting, however, might lead to discussions he would rather avoid. He hesitated, but the man's congeniality tipped the scales. "Sure. We can talk."

"Excellent. Come find me when you've finished your meal."

The two men shook hands.

As Kyle and Sketch stepped away, Reid realized that he would have to call Allison and reassure her that work was taking longer than anticipated and that he would be home in due time.

Reid sat facing the executive director across a back-corner table. The plastic tablecloth had been folded up and taken away. The indigent throng had thinned. Many of the volunteers had departed as well, having finished their cleanup duties. The few that remained were out of earshot. "Tell me about the mission," Reid said.

"Not much to tell." Kyle rested his forearms on the bare table. He wore the cuffs of his shirt sleeves rolled up to three-quarter length. "We've been serving the community almost seventeen years now. We have a paid staff of three: Me; Brandon, who made the announcements; and Jenny. She's the one who led the singing.

"Brandon is our outreach coordinator. Jenny, besides being our chief chef, is my administrative assistant. That's our code phrase for jack-of-all-trades. She pretty much does everything that needs doing. We also have fifteen to twenty volunteers. Some come more regularly than others, but they all serve."

"And the guy who gave the message?"

"That's Pastor Franklin Martel. We call him Marty. He shepherds the New Faith Chapel, a small nondenominational church on Birch Road. It's right on the boundary where East Palo Alto butts up against

Menlo Park. He volunteers his time when he can as do several local pastors."

"Sounds like quite an operation," Reid said. "Have you been with the mission from the beginning?"

"No. It was started by Walter Jenkins. I came on board about ten years ago, right after Walt died. He was a good man." Kyle eased forward at the waist. "So tell me about yourself. What's your story?"

"What makes you think I have a story?"

"Everyone has a story. Besides, you're here. To me that's significant because you're about as out of place as a lamb in a wolf's den."

"Is it that obvious?"

"Oh yeah."

Reid flushed. "So tell me about the men who come here."

"Nearly all the clients we serve are emotionally scarred one way or another. Their psychological wounds trap them in a spiral of hopelessness and despair. They get so caught up in reliving the past they can't get on with living their lives. We help them build a new foundation—a firm footing upon which they can start over, hence the name Bedrock."

"I was wondering about that."

"We believe Christ Jesus is the rock upon which men's lives can be rebuilt. Are you a believer?"

"No," Reid declared emphatically.

"I see. I also see that you're wearing a wedding ring. Not many homeless people do, you know."

Reid winced; this was a third oversight to expose his masquerade.

"So you are married, right?" Kyle pointed at the ring.

Reid considered lying until it occurred to him that any falsehood would be pointless. After ten years ministering to the chronically dysfunctional, the man would no doubt spot a deception immediately. "Yes, I am married."

"Happily?"

"Yes."

"Tell me about your wife."

"Why all the questions?"

"Our goal is to help people find the answers they seek. We can't do that if we don't know who you are."

"What gives you the impression I'm seeking answers?"

"Again, because you're here. You came to us."

"Not of my own volition. Sketch virtually dragged me through the door."

"Did he? So it must have been providence—interesting." Kyle paused as if considering the implications. "What is it that you seek, I wonder—vengeance, retribution?"

Reid startled. The man's perceptiveness had caught him off guard. "Yes. I mean, no. Well, I did, but no longer. Not by my own hand."

"Want to tell me what happened?" A gentle smile formed on Kyle's face. "Don't hold back. You're safe here."

The compassion in Kyle's eyes touched Reid at the core of his being. He felt himself unable to resist.

As he began speaking, the words came faster and faster. He described his relationship with his son and the distractions of being a self-made man. He talked about his desire to be a better father and how he had failed to bring his resolve to fruition.

He described Connor's murder and the horror that had gripped his heart. He told about hunting for his son's killer and the hatred that had driven him.

He finished by describing his confrontation in the homeless camp and how he had come within a hair's breadth of ending another man's life. When he was done, tears were spilling from his eyes.

Kyle listened without interrupting; his attention focused as if he were measuring every word. When Reid finished, Kyle sat back for a time as if reviewing what he had heard. At length, he leaned forward and laced his fingers together in front of him. "It's not vengeance you seek."

"What is it then?"

"It's forgiveness. You're under the false impression that bringing justice to the man who killed your son will take away your pain. It won't. Only when you are forgiven will you be at peace."

The truth underlying the executive director's analysis rang like a clarion in Reid's mind. In a rush, he recognized what he had been so desperately craving. Without realizing it, he had blamed himself for Connor's death. More to the point, he blamed himself for having failed to connect with his son's life. The tears flowed even more fiercely.

When the outpouring of grief subsided, Kyle said, "Now that you know what it is you seek, what will you do about it?"

"What do you mean?" Reid asked, drying his eyes.

"I could say I forgive you and mean it with all sincerity, but I doubt that my benediction would count for much. If you speak with your wife, it's possible she might bring you some comfort but not absolution. Your son is gone, so you can't obtain forgiveness from him, though I expect he would have forgiven you if you'd asked."

"How can you know that?" Reid snapped.

"Because of how you described your relationship. Clearly, you loved your son, though you might not have expressed it well. Kids can tell when their parents love them. No, I was thinking that you should talk to someone who has the authority to forgive absolutely."

"You mean God?"

"I do. But before you approach Him, you need to prepare yourself."

"Prepare myself? How?"

"The scriptures are clear. We must forgive before we can be forgiven. You will never find peace until you forgive the man who killed your son."

"Never!" Reid resolutely shook his head. "How am I supposed to do a thing like that, assuming it's even possible? The killer took everything from me—everything that's important. He destroyed whatever chance I might have had to be a good father. And you ask me to forgive him? Never. I can't."

"I'm not the one who's asking. I'm merely repeating God's ground rule: 'He who does not forgive will not be forgiven.' The choice is yours."

"Why has God done this to me?" Reid groaned.

"God didn't kill your son. Surely you must know that."

"Then why did He allow it to happen?"

"That I do not know, but I have faith that eventually you'll have your answer. After all, tonight you've learned what it is you seek. That's a good start."

With a heavy heart, Reid drove home to Menlo Park. Kyle Long's insights had touched a nerve. What troubled him most was the degree to which self-loathing had fueled his anguish.

Guilt was the soil in which his grief had taken root. But forgiving to be forgiven, how was that possible? How could he ever forgive the man who had murdered his son in cold blood? It was a requirement too far.

7

AGONY

Early April 2017

Two weeks after killing the man he had merely intended to rob, Ruben Walker was still horribly sickened by the magnitude of the crime he had committed. Rarely had he ventured away from his hiding spot and then only at night to scrounge food from trash bins and dumpsters. He had deliberately avoided all human contact.

To his amazement, the abandoned freezer in which he had chosen to shelter had turned out to be an agreeable place of refuge. Surrounded by weeds and tilted on its side behind an abandoned house, the freezer was visible only from inside the surrounding fence. From behind, it appeared to be nothing more than a junked appliance. Only from the front and with the lid upraised could a curious intruder recognize a squatter's camp.

The backpack Ruben had pilfered from his fourth foster home was still in his possession, and it still served as a lumpy pillow at night. While prowling the streets, he had picked up a few other necessities: a moth-eaten blanket, a plastic jug for storing water, a rusted pocketknife, and a nearly empty butane lighter. As for staying warm, even a rag of a blanket was better than wrapping legs and torso in old newspapers.

Upon first discovering the butane lighter, he had envisioned using it to set a campfire ablaze. Warm grub would surely be more palatable than the cold leavings that had turned his stomach. But then he had changed his mind. Even a small flame would attract unwanted notice.

During his first several nights, Ruben had slept not a wink. He had lain with eyes open, visualizing again and again the young man he had killed and the neat round hole in his victim's forehead. But to his dismay, he had soon discovered that the wound was all he could remember.

Again and again, he had struggled to picture the young man's face, but the park had been too dark, and everything had happened so fast. In his mind's eye, all he could see was a featureless blur and then a splatter of blood.

Each gust of wind, each noise in the dark had caused him to flinch in fear. At any moment, he had expected the police to descend upon his hideaway and haul him off to jail. But the wind was just the wind, and the fenced-in backyard had remained an island of refuge. There had been no sirens, no flashing red-and-blue lights, no police with guns drawn demanding that he flatten himself on the ground with arms extended.

Tormented during his nocturnal vigils, Ruben had tossed and turned while considering his crimes. There could be no denying that he had committed a terrible wrong and that his actions were worthy of absolute condemnation.

His motives, however, had seemed more problematic. Despite his misdeeds, he still dreamed of reuniting his family, and he again promised himself that one day he would see his dream fulfilled, assuming he could avoid being put in jail for the rest of his life.

The guilt that had shredded Ruben's soul had sparked within him a burning resolve to never commit another dishonest act. He promised himself that he would take to heart the lessons his mother had tried to teach: Stealing was wrong. Murder was wrong. They were to be eschewed at all cost. To the depths of his being, he lamented that he could not go back and undo the injury he had caused.

By the second week, Ruben's anxiety had begun to ease; and though he still feared being captured, his dread was less immediate. Feeling less threatened, he had ventured out more frequently and across a wider range. At first, he had avoided every human contact, but eventually, necessity had put an end to his excessive caution.

He was losing weight. Worse, he was weak and depleted. To gain the nourishment he needed, he would have to put money in his pocket. That meant he would have to find work somewhere.

At the beginning of the third week, Ruben climbed out into the morning air. Stiff and sore, he stretched to relieve the various aches induced by the freezer's enameled walls. Perhaps a discarded mattress should be his next item of salvage.

As he warily scanned the backyard, Ruben imagined how his day would go. First, he would visit a filling station and use their restroom to clean up as best he could. He reasoned to that the better his personal hygiene, the better his chances of landing a job. Next, he would search for recently discarded newspapers, hoping to chance upon a listing for an odd job that needed doing. With luck, he would find work as far away from East Palo Alto as he could travel on foot. It would be risky being seen in public, but his hunger told him that he was running out of other options.

Beyond these measured goals, his plans were sketchy. He hoped he would still be a free man at the end of the day—but one with a little money in his pocket.

Ten days later, Ruben was slamming a posthole digger into the loamy earth on Mrs. Unger's estate. The elderly widow had placed an ad seeking the services of a day laborer. Her desire was to have a decorative post-and-rail fence set in to protect her huge flower garden.

For Ruben, the job had seemed ideal. Tools and materials were to be provided. The work would be physically taxing but not exhausting. And the pay would be $7.50 an hour with a bonus if the task could be completed within two days.

After discovering the ad, Ruben had called immediately by begging the use of a landline at a filling station. To his amazement, the job was still available, and Mrs. Unger had agreed to interview him the following morning.

For Ruben, landing an interview had created a new problem: how to get from East Palo Alto to the eastern edge of Redwood City, where Mrs. Unger lived approximately a mile from the bay. He had considered walking, but even jogging would've taken too long, and he feared losing the opportunity to put some coins in his pocket. After analyzing his problem thoroughly, he ignored his self-imposed prohibition against mingling with other people and hitched a ride.

Mrs. Unger had turned out to be a dour woman with a grandmotherly smile. Ruben had judged her to be in her early eighties, though he lacked experience when it came to guessing the age of old folks.

She wore her long gray hair drawn into a ponytail. While conversing, her tendency was to absentmindedly massage her knuckles, which were swollen with arthritis. All in all, she had seemed like a pleasant lady who enjoyed talking, especially about her dead husband.

At first, Ruben assumed he was to be dismissed out of hand—a poor disheveled kid with no education and few social skills. His clothes were grubby and rumpled, and his hair in disarray. He had done his best to spruce up, but having lacked the proper toiletries, he had failed dismally.

Mrs. Unger, for her part, had seemed most bothered by her potential employee's confession that he had no experience whatsoever, not to mention that when pressed for references, he had admitted that those too were in short supply or rather nonexistent.

At length, however, she relented. After leading him to the site where the fence was to be installed, she pointed to the materials and the tools.

"How would you proceed?" she asked, and then she listened soberly while Ruben laid out the plan forming in his head. At length, she curtly declared that he was to be hired, which probably had as much to do with her sympathetic nature as with anything else.

As the sun arced higher in the sky, Ruben struggled to maintain the pace he had set for himself in the cool of the morning. Straightening up, he regarded the work he had already completed. Three fence posts stood upright, their rails attached.

Ruben had decided to nail on the rails as he went along. His other option would have been to set the posts first and pray that his measurements had been accurate and that the rails would reach from one post to the next.

With hardly a cloud in the sky and the day heating up, Ruben shed his T-shirt and used it to wipe perspiration from his brow. He then cast the T-shirt aside and finished digging the hole he had started. When the hole was deep enough, he wrestled in a fence post standing it upright.

After reconfirming its distance from the previous post and its height above ground, he tamped down a modest amount of earth around the base. He then used a level to straighten the post until it stood exactly vertical.

Next, he filled in the rest of the hole and packed the dirt down securely. After nailing on a pair of rails, joining the new post to the previous one, he stepped back to admire his handiwork. The fence was taking shape, and he was doing a good job. It was time to take a break.

Ruben slid the framing hammer he had been using into his belt and headed for the side of the house where he had previously taken note of a water spigot. As he passed beneath an open window, he could hear Mrs. Unger puttering inside. He wondered what she was up to—cleaning perhaps or maybe working on a craft project. He advanced soundlessly so as not to alert her. It wouldn't do if she were to conclude he was slacking off.

As Ruben approached the spigot, a white police cruiser with parallel blue-and-green stripes running along both sides pulled into the front driveway. The light bar atop the cruiser's roof began flashing red and blue.

A beefy man wearing a dark blue uniform clambered out. A gold shield glimmered on his chest. His hand clutched the grip of a large pistol holstered at his side.

"You there," the man bellowed, "show me your hands. You stay right where you are. Don't you dare move."

Taken by surprise, Ruben's immediate instinct was to turn and flee.

Having grown up on the streets, experience had trained him that the best way to avoid trouble was to get away as quickly as possible. But then he froze, his limbs paralyzed by the terror clawing at his mind. The memory that he was a wanted man literally locked his joints in place.

His worst fear was about to be realized. Somehow the police had tracked him down. They had found him. He would be arrested and sent to prison for the rest of his life. The whole world would soon know what he had done. He would never be reunited with his siblings. By the time he again thought about running, it was too late.

The man drew his pistol. Sliding into a two-handed grip, he pointed it directly at Ruben. "I told you to stay put. Don't you even twitch. Keep your hands where I can see them. What are you doing sneaking around Mrs. Unger's house?"

Aware that he was on the verge of being shot, Ruben forced himself to stand completely still. "I wasn't sneaking. I was getting a drink of water." He inclined his head toward the spigot.

The man tensed. "I told you not to move. Put your hands on your head. Interlace your fingers."

"What?"

"Are you deaf? Put your hands on your head. Lock your fingers together. Do it now."

As the scope of his predicament continued to sink in, Ruben became increasingly alarmed. For a space, it felt as if his brain had ceased to function. He had trouble grasping what the man was saying. He heard the words but couldn't tease out what was being demanded of him. He began to tremble.

"I'm not going to tell you again," the cop said. "Put your hands on your head. Lock your fingers together."

Ruben's gaze darted around frantically as he hoped to chance upon a means of escape. The realization came to him that he could easily outrun this enemy, who was at least forty pounds overweight. Yet attempting to outrun a bullet would be foolish in the extreme. But what other choice did he have? If he let himself be taken into custody, he would spend the rest of his days in jail. He prepared his body to flee.

"What's that stuck in your belt?" the man growled. His mood became even more menacing.

"It's a hammer," Ruben replied.

"And just what d'you plan on doing with that? You gonna bash somebody's head in?"

"No. I—"

"What's going on?" demanded a voice at Ruben's back.

He swiveled his head just enough to see Mrs. Unger emerge from around the corner of the house.

The elderly woman had donned a kitchen apron over her blue-and-white polka-dot dress. Her hands were white with a dusting of flour as if she had been interrupted while baking.

"Homer, is that you?" she exclaimed. "Why are you pointing a gun at this nice young man?"

As Ruben's thoughts became more organized, he noted the emblem on the cruiser's door and the lettering beneath it: Belvedere Homeowners Association. A closer inspection of the man's uniform suggested that he was a security guard, a rent a cop, not a real policeman.

"I caught this guy sneaking around beneath your window," Homer declared with an element of pride. "Obviously, he's up to no good. Look, he's got a weapon."

Mrs. Unger advanced until she stood beside Ruben. She glanced down at the hammer tucked into his belt. "Don't be silly. I'm letting him use that to build my fence."

Homer kept his pistol trained on Ruben. "You know this guy?"

"I most certainly do." Mrs. Unger smiled. "I hired him just this morning to set a fence in around my flower garden. Now put your gun away before someone gets hurt."

The security guard looked around with an air of uncertainty as if he was reluctant to accept that he was about to be deprived of the satisfaction of having nabbed a dangerous felon. At length, he holstered his firearm and stood fully upright. As he squared his shoulders, he gave a nod as if declaring that he had done his duty. "If you're willing to vouch for him, I suppose that's good enough for me."

"Thank you for being so reasonable, Homer," Mrs. Unger said with more than a hint of sarcasm. "At our next homeowners association meeting, I'll make a point of mentioning your diligence."

The security guard beamed with pride. His grin faded when he realized her accolade might have a double meaning. Still sporting a look of uncertainty, he climbed back in his car, switched off the light bar, and drove away.

Mrs. Unger turned to face her employee. "You're trembling. There's no reason to be afraid of Homer. He's more bluster than bite. Are you hungry?" She smiled warmly at Ruben.

"I don't—" Ruben struggled to make sense of what had just happened. He had come within a hair's breadth of being apprehended or even shot. But suddenly the threat was gone. How was that possible?

"I've got a batch of Toll House cookies baking in the oven. Would you like some? Or how about a ham and cheese sandwich? You look as if you could do with a decent meal. Come with me. We'll get you cleaned up, and you can forget all about this ugly incident."

Still shaken by the encounter, Ruben meekly followed Mrs. Unger into the house.

After washing his hands and face in the guest bathroom and drying them on an impossibly soft towel, Ruben climbed up on a tall stool at the kitchen counter. His gaze took in his surroundings, and he realized that he was in perhaps the finest house he had ever visited.

The furnishings were clean and well-ordered. The rooms were bright and tastefully decorated. More to the point, everything looked seriously expensive.

As Ruben balanced atop the stool, he remembered that his T-shirt was still draped over a fence rail beside the flower garden. Being half naked made him feel terribly self-conscious.

How, he wondered, *had he come to such a state of affairs visiting in a stranger's home unclothed from the waist up?* Feeling out of place, his initial instinct was to flee.

As before, something persuaded him to stay put, perhaps Mrs. Unger's lighthearted chatter as she prepared his lunch.

The old woman's voice seemed agreeable enough, but he paid little attention to her words. Instead, he fought to process the scenario that had just unfolded. Was the encounter a harbinger—a reminder that he would always be a heartbeat away from being apprehended?

He found the prospect demoralizing. The thought of being constantly hunted set him trembling again. He felt perhaps he should confess his crime then and there and put an end to running.

Suddenly Ruben realized his hostess had stopped speaking. She was looking directly at him. "I'm sorry?" he stammered, unsure what had transpired. He wondered anxiously if he might've uttered something aloud.

"I asked if you'd like mustard on your ham sandwich?"

"Sure." Ruben forced a smile and did his best to calm his nerves.

"Are you all right? You seem truly distressed, but then I suppose I would be too if someone had just pointed a big gun at me and threatened to shoot. You don't have to worry about Homer. He won't bother you again. It's just that this community is on edge, what with all the violence that's been going on. I swear I don't know what this world is coming to. By the way, is American cheese okay? I'm afraid I don't have cheddar."

"What?"

"For your sandwich—"

"Sure. American is fine. Thank you. You know, I really should get back to work. I'm hoping that maybe I can finish your fence today."

Mrs. Unger chuckled. "There's no need to be in such a hurry. It's not like the flowers are about to escape from the garden. Besides, it's a pleasure to have someone to talk to." She glanced through the door that led to the living room.

Ruben's eyes tracked her gaze and noted the silver-framed portrait of an elderly gentleman prominently positioned on the piano. He assumed the man must be Mrs. Unger's late husband.

The old woman continued, "Since Ralph's passing, I hardly have anyone to visit with, except on bingo nights at the church. Chips and a pickle?"

"Yes please." Ruben suddenly remembered that he was literally starving. The realization that he was about to enjoy his first decent meal in weeks helped ease his distress. "You have a nice home. Have you lived here long?"

Mrs. Unger drew a thumbnail sketch of her history as she served Ruben his lunch. He was intrigued to learn that long ago, she had been a junior high teacher.

Ruben's mother had always maintained that talking with educated people could advance one's own education. Yet he asked only a handful of questions as he ate with deliberate intensity. Mrs. Unger, for her part, seemed content to carry on the bulk of the conversation by herself.

By the time Ruben finished his ham sandwich, chips, pickle, and half a dozen Toll House cookies, he was feeling seriously full. "That was great," he declared with sincerity. "Now I need to get back to work. Your fence won't build itself."

Mrs. Unger glanced out the window toward the garden. "I doubt you'll finish today. You will be back tomorrow, won't you?"

"Only if you promise that cop won't return." Ruben gave an uneasy laugh to take the edge off his uneasiness.

Mrs. Unger chuckled as she touched a finger to her nose and then pointed at Ruben. "I'll make sure he stays away."

As the sun descended toward the horizon, Ruben looked back at what he had accomplished. He was a little over two-thirds done.

It was a good day's work, especially for someone unaccustomed to manual labor. He then looked toward the house and noted Mrs. Unger watching him through the kitchen window. She smiled when their eyes met.

Ruben decided he liked her very much. Even so, it wouldn't do to let her get too close. If she knew the sin he had committed, her opinion of him would shift in a heartbeat.

Several times while they had talked, she had asked about his history and his family. Twice, he had inadvertently let small details slip. Tomorrow he would be more careful. He would have to learn to be always on guard and avoid letting himself be drawn into sharing personal information.

Rather than chance an encounter with a stranger, Ruben decided to walk all the way home. His belly was full, but his pockets were still empty. He would be paid when the job was done.

Still, it had been a good day despite having nearly been arrested. *Odd how quickly a dude's fortunes can turn*, he thought.

Six weeks after constructing Mrs. Unger's fence, Ruben found himself back in East Palo Alto hanging out in an alley behind an all-night diner, waiting for the kitchen staff to dump the evening's garbage.

Scrounging through restaurant trash cans immediately after closing time was a trick he had learned from Silas Henry, a kid his own age. They had met on the streets ten days earlier.

Reluctant at first to strike up a friendship, Ruben had warmed to Silas gradually. That Silas's story was like his own had helped quell Ruben's apprehension.

Like Ruben, Silas was a virtual orphan, having been abandoned by his father after his mother's unexpected death; and like Ruben, Silas was a fugitive from the law, though so far, he had staunchly refused to discuss the nature of his misdeeds.

"It won't be long now." Silas kept a sharp eye on the restaurant's back door while he lounged in the darkened alley; his back braced against a cinder block wall. "They're busy tonight. There should be some good leavings." The boy spoke with what Ruben had come to regard as false bravado and an artificial show of confidence as if he needed to be firmly in control of whatever circumstance might happen to overtake him.

"Good" was all Ruben uttered in reply.

In truth, he was again slowly starving to death. The money he had earned by putting in Mrs. Unger's fence was gone, though he had tried to conserve every penny.

More than two dozen times, he had hustled odd jobs only to be rebuffed because someone else had already been hired, he had lacked the necessary skill set, he was too young, or his credentials had failed to pass muster—the latter being a polite way of telling him that street urchins needn't apply. After a time, the rejections had become so onerous he had simply quit looking. Instead, he had returned to panhandling and scrounging through garbage bins for whatever he could find.

The back door to the restaurant opened. A busboy wearing a white apron smeared with food emerged.

The kid was big. Ruben guessed his weight at more than two hundred pounds. He hefted a drawstring trash bag in each hand.

Stepping to the dumpster, he lifted the lid; but before depositing the bags inside, he ripped each bag open and scattered its contents atop the rotting garbage that was already there. He then reached down beside the trash bin to fetch an open can of motor oil, which he liberally poured out over the refuse.

The busboy then returned to the rear door, but he hesitated before disappearing inside. Peering into the darkness toward where Ruben and Silas stood waiting, he snarled, "Ain't nothing for you here, and there ain't gonna be. You vermin need to scat. We don't want you troubling our customers. Understand? If we catch you out here again, we'll call the cops. Now beat it." The back door slammed shut behind the busboy as he returned to his duties.

Ruben and Silas lingered a moment, making certain that the busboy would not return. They then rushed to the dumpster, hoping to salvage even a scrap of nourishment, but the motor oil had been too thoroughly applied. Nothing seemed edible, though Ruben felt compelled to sample a scrap of bread to make sure.

Silas stopped him. "It'll make you sick." He turned and began walking away. "Forget this place. Come on. Let's give Mike's a try over on Fourth Street. He's not as busy at night, but at least he doesn't pour crap over his crap. What do you say, Quick?"

Quick was the street name Ruben had chosen for himself.

One night after dinner while still living with his family, he had snagged the last cookie on the plate, and Travis had commented, "Man, you're quick." The appellation had taken root in Ruben's mind.

Ruben fell in behind his newfound friend. Ever leery, he kept an eye out for danger. The memory of the rent-a-cop's gun pointed at his chest was still fresh in his mind, but the streets were mostly deserted.

"Do you ever miss your brother?" he said as he trailed along.

Previously, Silas had let slip that he had an older brother, but he subsequently had refused to divulge anything about their relationship.

"No." Silas stopped, picked up a rock, and hurled it at a stray cat hunting mice in the alley. He missed.

Is Silas telling the truth? Ruben wondered. *Could he really have no desire to see his older sibling again?*

The notion seemed impossible, highly improbable at best.

On three occasions, Ruben had done what he could to track down his siblings, to no avail. Needing to maintain a low profile while searching for them had seriously hampered his efforts.

Ruben admitted with dejection, "I miss my sister and my brothers, especially Travis. He's nearer my own age. I guess we had more in common."

Silas halted and spun around to face Ruben. "What makes you think I care? Did I ask about your family?"

"No."

"That's right, no. So let's not be trading mushy memories about how good things used to be. It only tears you up inside."

They walked on in silence for several blocks. At length, they headed down an alley toward the rear of Mike's Diner. No sooner had they entered the alley than a squad car appeared at the opposite end, cruising slowly in their direction.

Without missing a step, Silas spun around and whispered, "Run."

Pumping his legs as fast as his weakened muscles would allow, Ruben managed to stay two paces behind his companion. When they turned the corner suddenly and without warning, Silas halted. It was all Ruben could do to keep from slamming into his friend's back.

Pointing up at the low-hanging fire escape attached to the side of a tenement building, Silas snarled, "Quick, give me a boost." He lowered his hands and shaped his fingers to resemble a stirrup, indicating what Ruben should do.

Perceiving straight away what was being asked of him, Ruben gave his friend a lift up. On their second try, Silas grabbed the retracted ladder, pulling it down.

Both boys scampered up to the first landing and immediately flattened themselves against its metal grating. Holding their breath, they watched the patrol car emerge from the alley and cruise past where they lay motionless.

As the cruiser vanished into the night, Silas whispered, "Cops are stupid. They never look up."

Ruben had noted that Silas tended to be a belligerent sort of individual even when circumstances called for a softer approach.

At times, he could be downright hostile. To Ruben, it seemed as if his acquaintance had constructed an emotional barrier between himself and the world around them—a shell to guard his heart.

Having already spent years on the streets, Silas was far more knowledgeable when it came to surviving in a threatening environment; but somewhere along the way, he had lost a chunk of his humanity.

The boys waited five minutes before warily climbing down from their perch. The metal ladder emitted a metallic shriek as it descended toward the pavement. A light flashed on in the window of the apartment nearest the lowest landing. Hastily the boys retreated to the alley from which they had escaped.

As they made their way toward the rear of Mike's Diner, they noted a trash truck hoisting bins skyward and emptying them into its belly. Regrettably, their efforts had been in vain.

"What do we do now?" Ruben asked with a growing sense of desperation.

Silas shrugged. "I can't think of any other places open this late. Come to think of it, Quick, we could head for the park. Picnickers sometimes leave the stuff they don't eat, but by now, most of the leftovers will have been picked clean. Shame it isn't dinnertime. Else we could head to the mission. They'd feed us for sure."

"What's the mission?"

"You don't know about the Bedrock? Man, you are green. The Bedrock Mission is a charity for homeless dudes. It's that way closer to downtown." Silas pointed to the east. "They serve dinner at six, but you have to get there before they close the doors. The chow is pretty good, but they have all kinds of rules, and they make you sing and pray. Which is why I don't go—less'n I must."

"What do you mean have to?"

"When pickings are slim, and I don't have a choice. Kinda like tonight."

"Do they go poking into your past?"

"You mean will they question you and then rat you out? No. They're cool that way. They figure a man's business is his own and nobody else's. But they will try to get inside your head."

"How?"

"It's hard to explain. Maybe tomorrow you should go and see for yourself. It'll broaden your horizons."

Ruben scowled. "What about tonight? I don't know how much longer I can go without eating."

"Me either, but the mission is closed, so there ain't nothing for it. Guess we'll just have to tough it out tonight."

"Well, if that's it then—" With a sigh of resignation, Ruben turned away and headed in the direction of the deserted house and the freezer that had become his home. "Maybe I'll catch you tomorrow."

Silas moved away toward his own destination but called back over his shoulder. "Not if you plan on hitting the mission, you won't. Hey, who knows, maybe you'll take a fancy to all that religious mumbo jumbo they throw at you."

Ruben wound his way along empty streets and dreamed of what it would be like to feast on a real meal again served by people who wouldn't press him about his past. So what if they were religious zealots? They could preach at him all they wanted so long as they served a decent spread.

8

ENCOUNTER

Mid-May 2017

Ten weeks after Connor's death, Reid pulled his Lexus to the curb and parked in front of Gavin Marsh's Menlo Park home. As he switched off the engine, he noted that the upscale neighborhood in which Gavin lived seemed deserted.

Only a few cars were parked on the street since most residents sheltered their vehicles in two- and three-car garages.

Reid sat for a moment, gazing out at the gathering dusk and wondering if whether he was doing the right thing.

On the verge of pressing the sport sedan's starter button, he hesitated and then drew his hand away. He needed answers, and there was only one man he trusted enough to help find them.

Gavin's home was the least flamboyant on the block. He could have afforded a larger place, but his frugal nature would not allow it. More than once he had declared that his two-bedroom Santa Fe–style ranch house with its adobe siding was perfect for his needs.

After climbing out of the Lexus, Reid headed up the front walkway. Out of habit, he activated the lock button on the car's keyless fob. The horn emitted a soft beep in response. Gavin opened the front door a few moments after Reid rang the doorbell.

Reid graced his friend with an apologetic smile. "Am I intruding? Maybe I should have called ahead?"

"You're kidding, right?"

"I know it's late, and I don't want to bother you if you're in the middle of something."

"Don't be ridiculous. I swear I don't know what's gotten into you lately." Gavin swung the door open wide. "Come on in. I just finished dinner, but there are plenty of leftovers. Are you hungry? It's spaghetti night."

"No, thanks. I just ate." Reid stepped inside.

Looking from the foyer into the living room, he noted that the house and its furnishings were immaculate as usual. In no way did Gavin fit the conventional profile of a confirmed bachelor. Consistently neat and fastidious in his appearance, dust and debris were to be viewed as a personal affront.

"Mind if we talk in the kitchen?" Gavin suggested. "I should finish cleaning up, and I assume you want a cup of coffee."

"Indeed I would." Reid followed his host toward the back of the house. "Sorry to barge in like this."

"Like I told you, it's not a problem. You are always welcome."

In passing, Reid noted the large hutch with its curved glass side panels that stood against the living room's east wall. He paused to take a closer look. "Am I mistaken, or have you added to your collection?"

"You have a sharp eye, my friend. Two pieces as a matter of fact," Gavin declared proudly. As an avid collector of Lalique glassware, he was always willing to show off his most recent additions.

The hutch contained a number of exquisite plates, bowls, and vases, plus several glass fish. "One is that amber vase with a perruche pattern."

"Perruche?"

"Lovebirds—parrakeets."

"Oh yes. Very nice." Reid had always regarded collecting fancy glassware an odd hobby, especially for a middle-aged man, but then to each his own.

"Regrettably," Gavin said with a sigh, "I missed out on an opalescent Calypso glass charger. For you uninformed, that's a plate with nude mermaids cavorting around the border. It was a rather stunning piece, but I messed up getting my bid in on time. Pity."

Gavin turned and continued toward the kitchen.

After washing the dishes and brewing a pot of coffee, he handed his guest a steaming mug. The two men then retired to the living room. Gavin sank down into his favorite recliner, where he did most of his reading. He propped his feet up on the ottoman. Reid sat on the Victorian love seat.

Rather than press his guest to discover what was on his mind, Gavin waited.

At length, Reid leaned forward and gazed across the room. "How's Charlie holding up?"

"He's hanging in there, but he sure doesn't have your finesse. The other programmers are beginning to resent him telling them what to do."

"But the integration is moving forward, right?"

"For the most part. I expect we'll finish on time or within a few days of our deadline."

"Where's the hang-up? I thought merging our subroutine with Berlman's navigation module would be a cinch. Why is there a problem?"

Gavin scowled. "If you'd spend more time at work, you'd know why. The issue is not with our software. The problem is getting cantankerous programmers to talk to one another. They work better together when there's a strong leader to guide them. A ship doesn't sail well without its captain."

"Maybe I have been neglecting my responsibilities, but there is a reason."

"Which I assume has something to do with you losing your son?"

"And that's why I wanted to talk to you."

Gavin waited for his friend to continue as if not wanting to add to Reid's distress by pursuing false assumptions.

"What happens," Reid said at length, "if God doesn't forgive someone?"

"Forgive what?"

"Whatever we've done wrong—our sins, I suppose."

"You mean what happens if we violate God's laws? I imagine the consequences might depend upon several factors." Gavin's eyes narrowed as he regarded his friend.

"Such as?"

"Well, for instance, the magnitude of the transgression. I imagine some offenses are more grievous than others, but don't get me wrong. All sins are evil and worthy of judgment in the sight of the Lord."

Gavin paused as if ordering his thoughts. "I suspect that when passing judgment, God takes into consideration our motives, as well as what's in our heart at the time. I believe sins committed with malice will be more harshly judged than those committed out of ignorance or due to negligence. I'm not sure if that answers your question."

"To a point. Does God judge everyone?"

"No. He judges only those who haven't entered into a saving relationship with His Son, Jesus. Those of us who are in Christ will never fall under God's judgment. The penalties for our sins have already been paid by Christ's death and resurrection."

"Sort of like a get-out-of-jail-free card?"

"More like an awesome gift we never could have obtained on our own."

"And for those who aren't in such a relationship?"

"Scripture says that their penalty will be eternal separation from God. They will spend forever in a place where God is not. The Bible refers to that place as Sheol. We call it hell."

"Someone recently told me that if we do not forgive, we will not be forgiven. Is this true?"

"It is. Matthew 6:15 explicitly states that if you do not forgive men their sins, your Heavenly Father will not forgive your sins. Where is this all coming from?"

Reid stood and began pacing the floor. "I met a man at the Bedrock Rescue Mission. His theory is that I blame myself for Connor's death and that I'm seeking forgiveness."

"Bedrock Rescue—"

"It's a charity for the homeless in East Palo Alto."

"What were you—"

"It's a long story. Maybe I'll tell you someday."

"You're going to keep me in suspense? So why would this guy think you're seeking forgiveness?"

"Over these last couple months, I've done a lot of soul-searching. When I think about how I treated Connor, it occurs to me that I gave him everything he wanted but little of what he needed. I wasn't much of a dad. I was too caught up in making my fortune. Perhaps that's why I feel the need to back off now as if somehow stepping away from work can make atonement."

"Too little too late, wouldn't you say?"

Reid bristled. "Gavin, you know one of the things I've always admired about you is that you never hold back."

"Sorry. I was just trying to point out that forsaking your professional responsibilities is unlikely to help."

"You're right. I guess in the back of my mind, I've been trying to earn forgiveness."

"And the forgiving others part?"

"There you go. There's my problem in a nutshell. How do I forgive the man who murdered my son? Is such a thing humanly possible?"

"Perhaps it's not humanly possible. Perhaps on their own human beings lack the capacity to forgive such a man."

"Great. So I'm screwed. What am I supposed to do?"

"You need to call upon the power of the Holy Spirit. You'll need God's help to let go of your hatred."

Reid stopped pacing and stared directly at his friend.

Gavin explained, "When we open our hearts and invite Jesus into our lives, He places His spirit within us. His spirit then guides and teaches us.

"Scripture is clear. It's the Holy Spirit that prompts us to follow the paths God has ordained. The spirit gives us the power to be obedient, to do God's will. Even more important, the Holy Spirit makes it possible for us to feel God's love. It's only by knowing the love of God that we can learn to love others, including the unlovable—those who have wounded us in unimaginable ways."

Reid sat down and buried his face in his hands. "I don't think I'm ready for this."

"Perhaps you should talk to God. Let Him help you work through your doubts."

Reid looked up. "Perhaps I will."

"I'm curious," Gavin said. "Tell me more about this Bedrock Rescue Mission. Who is this guy you've been talking to?"

"His name is Kyle Long. He's the managing director. He has an odd way about him. It's like he knows what you're thinking even if you're not actually thinking it. He and the rest of his staff serve an evening meal for the homeless. Altogether, I've been back about half a dozen times. Don't ask why.

"On my third visit, Kyle suggested I might want to volunteer. He said it would help me on my journey whatever that means. I agreed, but so far all, they've had me do is talk with some of the clients. That's what they call the homeless who frequent the place."

"You? You've been volunteering at a rescue shelter? Now that is remarkable."

"Why would you think so?"

"Serving the homeless—that's something I never would have pictured you doing."

"Me neither, but it has been enlightening."

"I'll bet you meet a lot of interesting people."

"More than a few. Last night, for instance, there was this young kid—still a teenager. He told me it was his first visit. He calls himself Quick. He wouldn't give me his real name. He's bright, mild-mannered, and introspective to a fault, not self-obsessed but more like thoughtful.

"He's also deeply troubled—fearful—reluctant to engage socially. In many ways, he reminds me of Connor. He's also perhaps the most disheveled human being I've ever encountered.

"His hair is a knotted tangle. His clothes are filthy, and he smells like he's been sleeping in a field. I must admit, he sparked my curiosity."

"Will you be seeing him again?"

"I doubt it. I could tell he was extremely uncomfortable about being there. It was all I could do to get him to just say hello."

Gavin lowered his feet off the ottoman and sat up. "You do realize I was serious about talking to God? You're going to need His help when you make your decision about His Son."

"What makes you think I'm going to make a decision?"

"Everyone does either overtly or by default. Look, if you want to talk more about how to go about this, let me know. I'm available."

"I appreciate that. I should be going. Allison will be worried if I don't get home soon."

"Does she know you've been volunteering at a rescue mission?"

"No."

"You haven't told her?"

"Like I said, it's a long story."

"And you think she won't understand? Or maybe you think she won't approve?"

"If you want to know the truth, it's embarrassing."

"Why, because you've trying to cope with the loss of your son? Don't you think she might be going through some of the same emotions, the same grief, the same feelings of hostility? Perhaps you could comfort her if you were to share your feelings and vice versa."

Reid made a sour face.

Gavin stood and accompanied his friend to the front door. "Keep in mind what I said about asking God to show you the direction you should go."

"I will."

Gavin called out as Reid traversed the path toward his car. "Will I see you at work tomorrow?"

"Probably," Reid called back, "but no promises."

Early on a Saturday afternoon, three days after speaking with Gavin, Reid was ambling at a deliberate pace along the San Francisco Bay Trail. Feeling the need for time alone to clear his mind, he had traveled north from Menlo Park.

Without consciously selecting a destination, he had gravitated to the Presidio and then to Torpedo Wharf.

The wharf, which juts out from San Francisco's northern coastline where the bay empties into the Pacific Ocean, afforded spectacular views of the Golden Gate Bridge. Looking up at the bridge's expanse high overhead, Reid paused to admire the panorama.

From where he stood gazing out across the water, he could see Alcatraz Island situated halfway to Oakland on the opposite side of the bay. It was a beautiful day, not a cloud in the sky, and the sun had just arced past the meridian. In another month, summer tourists would throng the West Bluff Picnic Area.

Most of the people Reid passed along the trail seemed to be in good spirits. His thoughts, however, were troubled and clouded.

At Gavin's insistence, he had spent several full days at work, putting out brush fires and encouraging employees to get along and stay focused. The task of integrating the synthetic reality subroutines was progressing more slowly than Gavin had implied. Yet with everyone working together, ERA would probably meet its deadline obligations but just barely.

Reid turned and continued walking. Gavin was right; a ship needs a captain. The problem was that when he tried to knuckle down and devote himself to the task at hand, his heart wasn't in it. Worse, his employees were noticing that he had lost his spark. Too often in meetings or while speaking with subordinates, he had caught himself stewing over distractions. Too often he had noted a look in their eyes that implied "If you don't care about the work I'm doing, why should I?"

Reid halted and gazed out at the bay. On impulse, he bent down to retrieve a large flat stone that lay beside the path. Drawing back his arm, he flung it toward the water. Being too heavy, the rock skipped only twice and then disappeared beneath the surface with a loud splash. He was out of practice.

With startling clarity, Reid suddenly pictured a similar sunny day. He and Connor had spent the afternoon at the Sand Dollar Marina. What had made the experience noteworthy was that it had been one of those rare occasions when he had intentionally torn himself away from work.

While walking along the shore, father and son had paused to engage in a rock-skipping contest. Reid's best effort had managed six skips. Connor, although only nine at the time, had managed seven. The boy's elation at having won their competition had been undeniable.

Without warning, Reid's eyes brimmed with tears. Other images of his deceased son flooded his mind, including the dreadful memory of finding his lifeless body in Drystone Park.

A wave of unbridled hatred rose within him. He picked up another rock and hurled it as far as he could. It sailed out into the bay and sank without skipping once.

"Connor," Reid sobbed, "I miss you. I miss you so much." He gritted his teeth and fought to restrain his emotions, but the tears still came. "Why?" he wailed softly. "What possible good can be served by your death? I don't understand. And why must I forgive the man who took your life—a man who deserves no mercy?"

As Reid's distress began to ease, he looked around. With embarrassment, he noted that a couple lying on a blanket nearby had been watching him. He nodded to indicate he was okay and moved on.

"Lord Jesus," he whispered as he plodded the trail, "if You're out there, I need Your help. I can't do this on my own. My agony is too great. If it's true You give Your spirit to those in need, then help me now. I beg You. Take this hatred from me and forgive me for what I've done and for what I haven't done."

An unexpected stillness settled over Reid. It came not as a soothing of his tangled emotions but as a glimmer of hope that his distress might pass.

He gazed out at the water. The ripples had lessened, and the surface seemed calmer. While staring at the bay, a more current memory came to mind. He pictured Allison as she had been before their marriage, and then he pictured her as she was in recent days. He found the contrast unnerving. How had he failed to notice a change so troubling? Had he been that distracted by his own grief?

A fresh patina of guilt enveloped Reid. In his efforts to cope with unimaginable loss, he had deliberately separated himself from his wife, leaving her virtually alone. As clear as day, he could number the choices that had diminished their life together. Rather than comfort his wife in her time of misery, he had forced her to fend for herself alone. No wonder their marriage was disintegrating.

A sense of resolve took root in Reid's consciousness. "Maybe I will never shed this hatred that burns within me. And maybe I will never regain the life I used to have. But I damn sure should be able to comfort my wife."

Reid turned and hurried back in the direction of the parking lot where he had left the Lexus.

An eerie quiet filled the Silver Vale House when Reid returned from San Francisco. Allison's Mercedes was in the garage. He assumed she was somewhere on the premises.

In a Ricky Ricardo voice, he called out, "Lucy, I'm home," but he received no reply. The stillness made him uneasy.

He checked the living room, the dining room, the kitchen, the downstairs bathrooms, the den, and the family room. All were deserted.

As he stepped out to search the backyard, he found Torus eagerly wagging his tail by the sliding glass door.

Reid scratched the scruff of the dog's neck. "No, old fellow, you stay outside. Maybe I'll bring you in later." Torus responded with a doleful whine as Reid slid the glass door shut and headed upstairs.

The master bedroom and the guest room were also empty. Opening the door to Connor's room, he found Allison lying fully clothed on the bed. She did not stir when he stepped inside.

Pausing for a moment, he assessed her breathing and was relieved to note that her chest rhythmically rose and fell. He eased closer. A ray of light tumbled through the window to paint the room with afternoon sunshine.

Looking around, Reid noted that the bedroom was just as Connor had left it. His high school mementos were still on his study desk. His clothes still hung in the closet. His acceptance letter to Stanford lay open on the dresser.

As Allison slept, her auburn hair spread out in lustrous flows atop Connor's pillow. Her features seemed less troubled than they had earlier that morning. How good it would be, he thought, if the serenity of slumber could endure during wakefulness.

He looked closer. Age had stolen the blush of youth from her cheeks, but in its place, he noted the elegance of a mature woman. He reached out and gently touched her shoulder.

Coming awake slowly, Allison blinked to clear her vision and then sat up. "You're home!" she exclaimed with surprise. "I thought you'd be gone longer." She self-consciously smoothed a collection of wrinkles from her blouse.

"Sorry. I should have texted you that I was on my way."

"No. It's fine." She glanced around the room. "I don't usually—I must have been tired."

Judging that he already knew the answer, Reid decided not to ask why his wife was sleeping in their deceased son's room. Instead, he said mildly, "You've been under a lot of stress. We both have."

As if coming fully awake, Allison swung her legs over the edge of the bed and sat up. "Did you find what you're looking for?"

"Not precisely, but I suspect the trip will turn out to have been worthwhile."

"I'm glad." Allison lifted her hand to cover a yawn. "What time is it?"

Reid consulted his watch. "Going on five thirty."

"I should start dinner. Are you hungry?"

"I could eat. Mind if I help?"

About to stand, Allison regarded her spouse with a startled look and sank back down.

Quickly Reid added, "Nothing bad is going on. I assure you. It's just that we need to talk. It's been too long."

"Definitely." Allison cocked her head as if measuring her husband's mood. "We're having lasagna. You can help by fixing the salad if you want."

"With Texas toast?" Reid suggested.

"If you'd like." Allison rose from the bed and headed downstairs, a puzzled expression on her face. Smiling, Reid followed.

Husband and wife sat at the oval table in the breakfast nook.

During the meal's preparation, they had spoken pleasantly but not about anything of substance. There was much Reid wanted to say, but he was having trouble figuring out where to begin. Rather than jump right in, he had decided to bide his time.

An opening of sorts came when Allison, looking past the kitchen and into the formal dining room, mused, "What do you suppose prompted us to buy this house?"

Reid swallowed a bite of lasagna and replied, "As I recall, we were pretty excited when it came on the market."

"An estate worthy of our social status, isn't that what we were thinking? But that's my point. How did we let ourselves become so beguiled?"

"I thought you liked this house?"

"I did at first. Now it's—overwhelming."

Reid set down his fork and sat back. "Overwhelming—"

"Spacious, roomy—hollow."

"You mean empty? Funny, I've had the same impression recently. The place seems so much larger since Connor died."

Allison stiffened.

With great tenderness, Reid continued, "It's time for us to face the reality that our son is gone. Avoiding the truth is tearing us apart, and for that I blame myself. It's been excruciating for both of us dealing with such a devastating loss. No wonder we shut down and turn away whenever the topic comes up."

For a time, Allison kept her silence, as if allowing the tension in her body to slowly ease. "Do you remember our housewarming party and how we left ourselves only one week to unpack and then how we had to hustle to put up the decorations?"

Reid chuckled. "I remember hiding unpacked boxes in the garage."

"What I especially remember is praying that the people we invited would become friends. True, a few did, but only a few and not close friends. When I think about our housewarming party, I'm reminded of our first apartment in Atherton. We were happy there. We knew our neighbors and enjoyed their company. What happened to us? Prosperity? Is that the ailment that afflicts us?"

"I think I understand. You feel isolated and abandoned. To put a name on it, I'd say you're lonely."

Bitterly Allison declared, "I'm past lonely. Like this house, I feel empty. When I look inside myself, the only thing I see is a great hollow filled with nothing. There's no joy, no sorrow, no anticipation, no regret—nothing except a huge void. I can't even grieve properly.

"And you, what do you have going on? You've never said. Why is that you've never spoken about losing our son? What is it that you feel inside?"

"Rage. A hatred so bitter it threatens to shred my soul. All I can think about is tracking down the man who killed Connor and ending his life as brutally as possible. It's tearing me apart inside."

"Is that why you've been staying away at nights? I know you haven't been working like you keep telling me. Twice, I drove by your office. Your car wasn't there. Once, I followed you when you left the house. When I lost you in traffic, you weren't headed toward ERA."

Reid flushed with embarrassment. "You're right. I haven't been honest with you. It's time you heard the truth."

Painfully he described his efforts to track down Connor's killer and the lengths to which he had gone. He talked about adopting the persona of a homeless man and what life on the streets was like. He described a few of the street denizens he had met, but he refrained from mentioning his encounter in the camp where he had nearly shot a man in the face.

He finished by saying, "For the last week and a half, I've been volunteering at the Bedrock Rescue Mission. At first, I thought there could be no better place to gather information than a shelter for the homeless. Lately, I've been going back for a different reason—one I can't completely explain—not yet. I know this sounds creepy, but because of my helping at the mission, I feel my hatred is starting to fade."

Allison listened as her husband recounted his activities. When he concluded, she said, "I knew something was afoot. I certainly didn't expect this."

"I hope you're not too angry."

"Like I said, I don't feel a thing. Do you plan to continue volunteering?"

"If you're okay with it, I'd like to—maybe twice a week. But I also intend to spend more time with you. It pains me to realize how far apart we've grown. I can't remember the last time we were intimate. We sleep in the same bed, but we might as well live on different planets. Don't you miss the sex?"

Allison nodded demurely. "What I really miss is being held. I used to love feeling secure in your arms."

Reid stood and opened his arms wide, an unequivocal invitation.

After hesitating briefly, Allison rose and let herself be enveloped by his embrace. The hug lacked the passion they had once shared, but it was a start, and for Reid, that was enough.

"Let me ask you something," he said softly. "Do you still believe in life after death?"

"I do."

"And you still put your faith in Jesus?"

"Yes," Allison said. "So did Connor. Knowing I will see him after the resurrection is the only reason I haven't done myself in."

"Connor was a believer? Why is it I never knew that?"

"Because he dreaded facing the ridicule he knew would come his way." Allison pulled back so she could look up into her husband's face. "Why bring this up now? You've never wanted to come near this subject before."

"Because I think I might be a believer too."

"What?" A slow smile emerged on Allison's face, replacing her look of astonishment. It was her first smile in months. "Tell me what happened," she prompted with enthusiasm.

Reid opened his arms, and they returned to their seats at the table. He recounted his introduction to Kyle Long and his subsequent conversations with Gavin, and then as best he could, he tried to capture the essence of his experience along the shoreline of the bay. In conclusion, he admitted, "It's too soon to tell what I really feel, but this is a good thing, right?"

"Most definitely."

"And that's why I want to continue as a volunteer at the mission— to see where it leads."

"Then I think you should, and I'll go with you if you'd like."

"Not yet. I need to do this on my own, but I'll keep you informed of everything that happens. Never again will I shut you out. You are my wife, and I love you."

"And I love you."

"We're going to get through this," Reid declared with determination. He took another bite of his lasagna, which had grown cold.

A larger crowd than usual filled the Bedrock Rescue Mission. Reid eyed his dinner tray as he sat across the table from his old buddy Sketch.

The evening's fare was tuna casserole, peas, and a freshly baked dinner roll. The rumble of scattered conversations filled the room. The casserole, Reid decided, was really good.

Sketch looked up from his dinner and, with his mouth full of food, said, "Any luck yet finding your son's killer?"

Reid swallowed. "None. It's been two months, and the police don't have a clue. I'm beginning to wonder if we'll ever catch this guy. By now, he's probably in another state or another country."

"He should be—if he has any brains."

"It's really weird," Reid admitted sheepishly, "but part of me is glad they haven't caught him yet."

Startled, Sketch's eyes went wide. "How can you say that? The guy killed your son?"

"I know, but recently, the pain of losing Connor has started to fade. I dread the thought of what'll happen when they catch the murderer—having to sit through his trial, reliving gruesome memories."

"If you're lucky, he'll resist, and they'll shoot him. You can always hope."

"I'm not sure I want that either."

"You did a month ago. What's changed?"

"I have, I think." Reid shrugged. "Let's not talk about me, okay? What about you, Sketch? What's your story? You've never told me. Why are you here?"

"For the grub."

"You know what I mean. What happened to you?"

The street denizen's eyes narrowed. "You really want to know?"

"I do."

Sketch put his fork down on his plate and leaned forward. "Why?"

"Because that's what friends do. They get to know each other."

"You want to be my friend?"

"If you'll allow it."

"Well, then—" Sketch turned his head to regard the man seated to his left.

No one was seated to his right. The man chose not to acknowledge Sketch's stare. Instead, he kept his eyes fixed on his dinner plate as if deliberately ignoring what was going on around him.

During his time on the streets, Reid had noted that many of the homeless were experts at minding their own business. Early on it had become apparent that a sure way to invite trouble would be to meddle in situations that were none of his business.

Apparently, satisfied that the man wasn't eavesdropping, Sketch returned his attention to Reid and said in a confidential whisper, "I was an architect—a damn good one. I built high-rise condominiums.

"My company was well-known in the industry. The last project I worked on was to have been my magnum opus—four residential towers surrounding a central quadrangle. Construction was state of the art—energy efficient—a self-contained community.

"A week after the grand opening, one of the towers caught fire. The cause was later determined to be a wiring fault. Seven people died. Sixty families were left homeless.

"I spent everything I had to compensate the survivors and their families. I lost my business, my license, and my reputation. Three months later, my wife, whom I loved with all my heart, died in a freakish accident. That was ten years ago, and here I am."

"I'm sorry." That was all Reid could think to say.

"I suspect most of these guys"—Sketch swept the room with his hand—"are here because they've lost something precious: their livelihood, a loved one, part of themselves."

"No doubt." Reid felt a tapping on his shoulder.

He turned his head to look up and found Jenny Townsend smiling down at him. "Sorry to intrude," she said, "but I need to speak with you. Have you got a moment?"

"Sure." Reid stood.

Jenny smiled at Sketch. "You don't mind, do you?"

"Not at all."

The mission's administrative assistant addressed Reid again. "Leave your tray. You can come back to it later, or someone will bus it for you."

Reid followed Jenny as she made her way through the kitchen and toward the business offices at the rear of the facility. She invited him inside one of the smaller spaces but left the door ajar. She indicated one of two metal-framed chairs. Reid sat down, but she remained standing.

Jenny looked down and said, "You've been with us, what, two weeks now? How do you feel it's going?"

"I think it's going well. Is there a problem?"

"Not at all. We've been pleased with your ability to relate to our clients. Not everyone can, you know. It takes a certain level of sensitivity."

"Actually I consider it an honor when they feel comfortable enough to open up."

"And well, you should."

"Thank you. So what did you want to talk about?"

"Two things actually." Jenny braced a hip against the secretarial desk. "We've been watching your approach, and for the most part, it's been more than satisfactory."

"But?"

Jenny folded her arms over her chest. "There's a reason our bodies scab over old wounds. If you keep picking at them, they fester.

"You need to tread carefully when probing a client's history, especially if you're ill prepared to cope with what turns up.

"Dredging up buried memories can do more harm than good, even to the point of driving a client to suicide. Sadly we've seen it happen. Don't get me wrong. We believe you would never intentionally harm a client. Just be aware. Proceed slowly and cautiously.

"When exploring a client's psyche, you never know what you're going to find. Some men might even become violent, particularly if they sense you're about to expose their most guarded secrets."

"You're referring to my conversation with Sketch, I presume."

"We can use him as an example, but no, he's not especially vulnerable. Sketch has far more insight into his psychological pathologies than most. Even so, he is poorly equipped to deal with the guilt he feels. He's in a stable state of equilibrium, but if the right stimulus were to come along, he could be pushed over the edge. What I'm saying is that Sketch has accepted his past but is unable to rise above it."

"I think I get what you're saying, and I consider myself warned, but how do you know if you're probing too deeply?"

Jenny nodded thoughtfully. "Good question. Mostly by experience, I suppose. Rule of thumb, if you're unsure, stop pushing."

"And what's the second thing you wanted to talk about?"

"Another warning but of a different sort. At all times, you need to protect yourself. Our clients might look helpless and vulnerable, but among their number, you'll find some of the best con artists you'll ever encounter. They've had years to practice scamming the unsuspecting.

"Oddly enough, the more compassionate you are, the more susceptible you become to their tales of misery and woe. Don't let them draw you in, especially if they ask for personal favors."

"Such as?"

"Such as cosigning for a temporary loan till they get back on their feet or seeking a ride to visit a sick buddy. Oftentimes they'll use that ruse to meet their dealer to buy drugs. They can be incredibly inventive. Just be aware that some of our clients will use you any way they can. And did I mention that they can be violent? Keep your eyes open. Maintain a high level of suspicion."

"Got it. By the way, how did you know what Sketch and I were discussing? Is the meeting hall bugged?"

"Absolutely not. Such a betrayal would destroy the trust we've worked so hard to earn."

"Indeed it would. Well, if the place isn't bugged, then it must be that you read lips."

Jenny blushed. "I'd appreciate it if you'd keep that thought to yourself."

"No worries." Reid tipped back in his chair. "Let me ask you something. What is Kyle's story? How did he wind up here? He seems like the kind of guy who could have had any career he wanted."

"I imagine he probably could have. Why do you ask?"

"For the same reason I was talking to Sketch—to get to know him better."

"I see. Well, as you might've guessed, Kyle was military—special forces, a sergeant. He served in Afghanistan. One day on patrol, his squad was ambushed. He lost five men. He blamed himself for not having foreseen the danger. It took a long while for him to deal with his losses. Ultimately, he learned that the best way to stop thinking about self is to serve others. This happened not long after he'd come to Christ. And then Walter Jenkins died, and the mission needed a new executive director. The rest you know."

"And you, what's your story?"

"Some other time." Jenny uncrossed her arms and stepped toward the door. "Sounds like dinner is winding down. I should be in the kitchen to supervise cleanup. Feel like washing some pots and pans?"

"Lead the way."

The city's night sounds greeted Reid as he exited through the mission's front door. He was feeling numb and depleted. It had been a long day, and cleaning up after sixty hungry vagrants had taken considerable effort.

Jenny Townsend accompanied him out onto the sidewalk. She was the last to leave. "Thanks for your help," she said as she turned to lock the front door. "It's amazing how much food these guys can pack away."

"Which reminds me," Reid said before heading off, "who pays for their meals? Where does the money come from to fund the mission?"

"Donations mostly. Churches in the surrounding communities are our biggest contributors. The city helps with special projects from time to time. Besides, not every indigent is penniless. Sometimes our clients contribute or leave bequests."

"Really?"

"Homelessness is as much a state of mind as a consequence of poverty. You'd be surprised at the resources some of our guys can draw upon." She gave Reid a knowing look.

"I never would have guessed." The color rose in his cheeks.

"Good night." Jenny turned away but then stopped and looked back. "Remember what I said. Keep your guard up when dealing with desperate men."

"I will. Say, would you like me to escort you to your car? It's late, and as you indicated, you never know what to expect."

Jenny smiled. "I appreciate the offer, but I'll be fine. People in this neighborhood know me."

"Be safe then."

"Shall do. Will you be back tomorrow?"

Reid gave a gesture of uncertainty. "I don't know. I'll have to see how my day goes."

"Okay. By the way, thanks for your help." Jenny turned and walked away with a confident stride.

"You're welcome," Reid called after her as he watched her go.

Interesting woman, he thought.

He found it easy to see why Kyle valued her skills. Not only was she competent; she was compassionate as well. She would have made an excellent sales rep.

He tried picturing her in the business world, calling on clients, making sales. Somehow the image seemed off kilter. He gave up and headed in the opposite direction, having parked his Lexus four blocks away in the lot of one of the big-box stores with its own security patrols.

Reid had traveled less than a hundred paces when he was startled by a noise nearby. A paroxysm of coughing had shattered the night's quiet. He looked around and noted a dark shape braced against the front wall of the hair salon across the street. At first, it was difficult to make out what the shape might be, but he soon realized it was a man curled up on the sidewalk as if he had collapsed in upon himself.

The cough came again, a wet, gurgling noise.

Reid strained to look closer. The man's features were obscured by shadow, though they seemed familiar. His first impulse was to hurry on.

Best not to get involved, he reminded himself. *Don't go poking your nose into matters that don't concern you.* But then his conscience began having its say.

Feeling conflicted, he looked closer. A flash of recognition drew him across the street. "Quick? Is that you? What are you doing lying here on the sidewalk? Are you well?"

It was a stupid question. Reid scolded himself.

Obviously, the kid was ill. His cheeks were flushed. There were dark circles around his eyes. A moist sheen glistened on his forehead and matted his ebony hair. Worse, he looked weak and helpless.

Quick spoke without looking up. In a husky voice, he murmured, "I tried to make dinner but was too late." His breathing seemed abnormally rapid. A paroxysm of coughing seized him again. When he spit, his sputum was tinged with blood.

Reid glanced around. There was no one nearby who could assist. He would have to deal with the situation on his own. He thought about simply walking away but then reached down to help Quick to his feet. The lad did not resist.

As Quick gained his footing, Reid noted that his clothes were even filthier than before, and his body odors no less pungent. "How long have you been like this?"

"A couple days."

While placing an arm around the boy's shoulders to steady him, Reid's hand grazed the side of his neck. His skin felt unduly warm. Clearly, he had a fever. "You may have pneumonia. We need to get you evaluated."

"I'll be fine," Quick protested.

"No, you won't, not without the right kind of treatment. Look, there's an urgent care clinic about half a mile from here. I'm pretty sure they're still open. I've driven past it several times on my way home. Do you think you can walk to my car? It's only a couple blocks. Or I can come back and get you."

"I can make it," the young man declared with defiance.

"Let's give it a try then." Reid supported his charge as they made their way to the Lexus. Twice, he had to keep the young man from falling when he stumbled.

"Why are you doing this?" Quick wheezed between labored breaths.

"Because you're sick. Come on. We're almost there. You can make it."

After settling Quick in the passenger seat, Reid drove with haste to the urgent care center.

9

RELATIONSHIPS

Early June 2017

A mild summer breeze chased away the thin veil of fog that had settled over Atherton during the night.

The city was just waking up as Reid pulled into the parking lot of the Bright Star Motel. The motel was only a ten-minute commute from his Silver Vale home, but it was thirty minutes, depending on traffic, from his offices at ERA.

Reid checked his watch. Were he to leave immediately, he would still be late to work. He chided himself for not having rolled out of bed the moment his alarm had sounded.

Three days had elapsed since Reid had dragged Quick to the urgent care center. The doctor had insisted upon admitting his patient to the hospital, but Quick had staunchly refused.

So after paying for his charge's outpatient treatment, Reid had settled Quick into the Bright Star. Consequently, for the past seventy-two hours, he had been doing double duty as corporate CEO and nursemaid.

Reid felt sluggish and mentally drained.

Is this what middle age is supposed to feel like? he wondered.

After gathering up a brown paper bag from the back seat, he locked the Lexus and headed to room 104.

Convincing Quick that he needed medical care had taken some doing. Had the young man been any less ill, he surely would have refused treatment. However, in that he was suffering from malnutrition and exposure, as well as from a raging lung infection, he had finally relented but not without protest.

Such stubbornness. Reid shook his head as he mentally recounted the contest of wills. *Why so reluctant?* he wondered, picturing again the apprehension obvious in the young man's eyes.

Reid knocked softly on the door. When he received no reply, he wondered if, feeling stronger, Quick might have fled.

To be sure, the young man's condition had improved remarkably over the past thirty-six hours. The antibiotics appeared to be doing their job. After knocking a second time with the same result, he used the duplicate room key the clerk had provided to quietly unlock the door.

Quick lay sprawled atop the bed, asleep. The sheet and thin blanket that partially covered him were in disarray, implying a restless night.

The magazines Reid had purchased lay scattered across the floor. Unsure of the young man's interests, he had selected titles on a variety of subjects, including hot rods, sports, and bow hunting.

Reid glanced at Quick's backpack, the young man's only apparent possession. The pack sat near the bed's headboard within easy reach. He again considered rummaging through the pack's various compartments to learn its secrets, but as before, he decided to respect the young man's privacy.

Trust, he reminded himself, *is difficult to win and easy to lose.*

Stepping fully into the room, Reid shut the door behind him. He quietly set the grocery bag down on the table by the window.

Remaining motionless for a time, he monitored the young man's respirations. His breathing was slower and less labored than before—clear evidence of a continuing recovery.

Quick stirred. His eyelids fluttered and then popped open in panic. Then as if recalling where he was and what had recently transpired, he seemed to relax somewhat. "What time is it?" he asked as he stifled a yawn. He sat up.

"A little after seven thirty in the morning." Reid bent down to gather up several of the magazines. He deposited them in a neat pile on the table. "How are you feeling?"

"Okay."

"Does your chest still hurt?"

"Not as much."

"I'm glad to see you're more alert. You've been pretty much out of it these last couple days."

Quick climbed out of bed. "Sorry, but I gotta take a leak." He had on boxer shorts and nothing else.

As he padded sleepily to the bathroom, Reid again noticed the scars and abrasions that marked the young man's body—evidence of a life subject to recurrent conflicts. Most apparent were the defensive wounds on his hands and forearms. Many looked recent. Obviously, life on the streets could be rough.

When Quick reemerged from the bathroom, he seemed more at ease. He crossed his arms self-consciously as he looked around. "Where are my clothes?"

"They were too filthy to salvage. I threw them out."

"Say what?" Quick's eyes narrowed as he glowered at Reid. "Man, you had no call to do that. Now what am I supposed to do?" In a huff, he plopped down on the end of the bed.

"Not to worry. I brought you some fresh duds." Reid stepped to the table and began fishing in the paper bag. He pulled out a striped cotton shirt, denim jeans, a pair of dark brown socks, sneakers, and a new pair of cotton briefs. "I'm sure these will fit. Go ahead. Try them on."

Quick eyed the apparel. "They look used. Where'd you get them?"

"They belonged to my son."

"Won't he be pissed when he finds out you took them?"

"I'm certain he won't object. Besides, I know he'd want you to have them. Go ahead. See if they're your size."

Quick carried the stack of clothes into the bathroom. When he came out, he looked halfway respectable.

Reid nodded. "Good. I thought you and he were the same size. All you need now"—he reached into the bag again and pulled out an electric razor, which he handed over—"is a shave and a haircut. As for the shave, this will help. As for the haircut, we can see to that later."

"Was this your son's as well?"

"No. I picked it up on my way home last night. It didn't seem fitting, making you use another man's razor."

"What makes you think I want to shave? Maybe I like the idea of growing a beard."

"Do whatever you like, but you'll get farther in this world if you make yourself presentable. Too often people judge others by their appearance."

"So I've noticed." Quick turned to face Reid, a look of suspicion in his eyes. "Why are you doing this—mothering me—bringing me all this stuff? What's in it for you?"

"You needed help. I saw an opportunity to do a kindness. What I get is the satisfaction of knowing I helped when help was needed. I also got you this." Reid reached into the bag and pulled out a cell phone, still in its original packaging.

"Man, you're a regular Father Christmas, but I can't take that. No way can I afford the fees."

"Not a problem. I set you up with your own account, and I've prepaid everything for six months. I figure by that time you'll be back on your feet. By the way, I've already programmed my numbers into the phone so you can call me anytime, day or night."

Quick eyed the phone with uncertainty.

"Look, it's just a gift, okay? Nobody's going to be tracking you. Nobody's going to be listening in on your conversations. It'll make your life easier. That's all. You might as well take it, since I don't have a use for it. If you don't plan on keeping it, you can sell it. Use the money to buy food or drugs or whatever."

"I don't do drugs," Quick snarled. "I ain't no druggie."

"Sorry. I didn't mean street drugs. I was thinking more along the lines of prescriptions like the antibiotics you're taking now. Speaking of which, did you take your pills this morning?"

"Not yet."

"How about taking them now so you don't forget? Remember what the doctor said. It's important to complete the entire course of treatment. Otherwise, you might relapse."

"Look, man, no matter what you might think, you ain't my mama. I can take care of myself. I don't need you telling me what to do and what not to do."

"Well, sure as hell, somebody should. When I scooped you up off that sidewalk, you were a mess. Is that what you call taking care of yourself? By the way, how old are you?"

"Eighteen."

Reid challenged the young man with a scowl.

Quick shrugged. "All right, I'm seventeen. Hey, don't be giving me that look. It's true. My birthday was in April."

"Fine. You're seventeen. And by the way, what's your real name? I know it's not Quick."

"Why should I tell you?"

Reid held his hands out, palms up. "Look, I get it. You have your doubts about me, but why not let me help? What have you got to lose? Everyone can use a friend now and then.

"Oh, I almost forgot. He reached into the brown paper bag again. I wasn't sure if you'd feel like being up and about today, so I stopped and got you some food—two breakfast burritos, taters, and a carton of milk. You should eat while they're still warm."

Reid set the bag containing Quick's breakfast out on the table. He then refolded the grocery bag and put it aside for later use.

Once more, Quick seemed to be on the verge of protesting, but he then changed his mind.

Apparently, hunger was more powerful a motivator than pride. He stepped forward, grabbed one of the burritos, and took a healthy bite.

Reid drew an envelope from the inside pocket of his sports coat. He laid it on the table. "There's some cash in here. It's not much, but it should cover a few of the things you need. Try to take it easy today. Okay? I'll stop by again this evening. Right now, I must get to work. This is a big day for ERA. That's the company I run. We've just finished adding our synthetic reality subroutines to Berlman Automotive's software. This is the day we get to show them the true power of our product. Wish me luck." He stepped toward the door.

"Good luck," Quick muttered as he chomped another bite of burrito.

As Reid fired up the Lexus, he glanced in the rearview mirror. Looking at the door to 104, he wondered what lay behind so much animosity. Was the young man's belligerence a mask, a ward to keep others from getting too close, a way to limit vulnerability? Only time would tell.

Dark clouds rolled across the sky as Ruben gradually made his way from Atherton to East Palo Alto. Casting an eye toward the heavens, he hoped the rain would hold off a little longer.

The decision to flee from the Bright Star Motel had been difficult. Physically depleted because of illness and weakened by a chronically poor diet, the easy choice would have been to stay and milk his benefactor's generosity for all it was worth.

His conscience, however, had balked by asserting that he was supposed be the master of his own destiny. Living off charity was for weaklings.

Ruben hefted his backpack to relieve the pressure of its straps on his shoulders.

The streets he traveled were becoming more familiar. He estimated that in another half hour he would reach his destination—the deserted house and the overturned freezer he had learned to call home. *Who would have imagined*, he thought to himself, *that such an unlikely hideout could feel so safe?*

As Ruben passed a shop window, he caught a glimpse of his own reflection out of the corner of his eye. He startled, thinking that a stranger was tracking his steps. Then he laughed when it occurred to him that he was wearing another man's clothes.

He stopped to admire his image. The cotton shirt with its button-down collar and the designer jeans brought to mind the affluent dudes who had strolled past on the street, never noticing he was there.

What would it be like, he wondered, *to own a closet full of such fine duds?*

Ruben looked up just in time to see a police cruiser turn the corner two blocks ahead and roll slowly in his direction. He hastily ducked into an alley and prayed that the cops hadn't noticed. He squatted down behind a dumpster and waited. The cruiser slowed as it passed the alley, but then it moved on.

After waiting to make sure the police were gone, Ruben breathed a sigh of relief. When he stood up, he felt a wet sensation at the side of the leg where his thigh had pressed against the dumpster. He looked down and saw a dark smudge on his pant leg. He cursed himself for having been so careless. Maybe he could wash the gunk off in a filling station restroom. He hoped it would not leave a stain. Or perhaps he should give up any notion of one day possessing a closet filled with nice clothes.

He headed off again at a faster pace. Twenty minutes later, Ruben turned onto the street that led to the abandoned house. Out of habit, he surveyed the surrounding neighborhood, making certain all was quiet. He noted that a car was parked at the opposite curb, but no people were in sight.

When he reached the backyard, he scurried over the fence. Dropping softly to the ground, he looked around again. The freezer was exactly as he had left it—tipped on its side with its lid closed. There was no indication his hideout had been disturbed.

Creeping forward slowly, Ruben propped the lid open with the stick he had fashioned. His blanket, makeshift pillow, and other meager possessions were where he had stowed them. He smiled at his good fortune.

Voices came from inside the house, and then someone opened a rear window. Ruben immediately ducked down behind the freezer. There was nowhere else to flee without being seen.

Snatches of conversation reached his ears. A man and a woman were discussing real estate matters—property taxes, easements, mortgage rates, and other issues he did not comprehend. A minute later, the voices faded and were gone.

Ruben recognized his opportunity to escape, but leaving would mean abandoning his place of refuge. He decided to stay put and see what would happen. A moment later, the back door opened, and three people stepped into the yard: two women and a man. Ruben ducked further out of sight.

"As you'll notice," said the mature woman wearing a pantsuit outfit, "the property needs considerable work, but the location is good, the roof is sound, and for the most part, the fence is still intact."

"How many homes are vacant on this block?" asked the man. He wore a gray blazer and a shirt like the one Ruben had on.

Ruben peeked around the corner of the freezer just as the second woman pointed in his direction. "What's that?"

"Looks like an old freezer," said the mature woman. "Whatever it is, we can have it hauled away." She began walking toward where Ruben was hunkered down. "I gather the previous owners were rather lazy. Seems it was easier for them to toss broken appliances into the backyard rather than truck them to the dump."

A rush of panic arose in Ruben. If he stayed put, he would surely be discovered. But if he ran, his hideout would be revealed, and he would lose all his possessions.

More than that, the man looked to be in good physical shape. Ruben figured that if push came to shove in a contest of strength, owing to his weakened condition, he would come out second best. Soon it became apparent that the only reasonable course of action was to run. He grabbed his backpack, his blanket, and his pillow and bolted for the fence.

Startled, the mature woman let out a shriek. The man tensed but did not pursue.

After scrambling over the fence, Ruben ran for several blocks. When he paused to listen for sounds of pursuit, the streets were quiet. He slowed his pace and continued walking toward downtown East Palo Alto. He remembered other places where he could spend the night, but none were nearly as satisfactory as his former refuge, which was now lost to him.

A thought came to Ruben. He halted and looked back. Maybe things weren't as bad as they seemed. Most likely the mature woman was a real estate agent showing an abandoned property to prospective buyers. But the house and the yard were in terrible shape. Perhaps the young couple would choose not to spend hard-earned money on such a dump. If so, they would go away and not return.

On the other hand, if they were in the market for a fixer-upper and they were to buy the property for that very reason, they would certainly be on the lookout for trespassers going forward.

With care Ruben debated both possibilities. At length, he was forced to acknowledge that his hideout's most appealing feature had been its seclusion, which had just been shattered. It was simply too dangerous to return and risk someone alerting the police. He set his feet toward downtown and continued walking.

A clap of thunder sounded overhead. When Ruben looked up, a raindrop struck him in the center of his forehead.

"Let's try over there," Silas Henry said, pointing to a trash can near the center of Grosvenor Park in East Palo Alto. He and Ruben had been gathering aluminum cans and bits of aluminum scrap for over an hour. They had gotten an early start, having rolled out of their fiberboard shelter well before dawn.

At first, Silas had refused to share his hideout, but he relented when Ruben explained the circumstances by which he had lost his own place of refuge.

Ruben also pointed out that by banding together they could better defend their lair. For Silas, the argument that there was strength in numbers seemed to make terrific sense. The one thing he feared most was to be set upon by thugs who preyed upon the indigent. Consequently, the two comrades in arms had spent the previous three nights huddled in their makeshift redoubt.

Ruben looked to where Silas was pointing. "Didn't we check that one already?" He was feeling listless and irritable. The chronic fatigue that plagued his life on the streets was again getting worse.

"Man, where is your head? We came into the park over there, remember?" Silas pointed. "That's the can we tossed."

"Got it." Ruben pushed the shopping cart they had fetched from a nearby supermarket toward the trash can.

As he trudged along, he recalled the brief time he had spent at the Bright Star Motel—the clean sheets, the hot showers, the respite from city noises. He also thought about the envelope he had left lying on the table. How could he have been so prideful? He hadn't even bothered to count the cash it had contained.

Foolishly he had turned his nose up at the gift simply because accepting charity meant you were less than a man. How idiotic.

"By the way, I've been meaning to ask," Silas said as he strolled beside the shopping cart, "how'd you get on at the mission? I assume you went, didn't you?"

"Yeah, once. No, twice, but the second time I was too late to get fed."

"What did you think of all that religious crap they shove at you?"

"It wasn't a problem. I kind of enjoyed some of it."

"For me," Silas sneered, "that stuff is like fingernails on a chalkboard. How can you like singing hymns and being preached at?"

"When I was young, before the twins were born, my mom used to take my brother and me to church. The singing reminds me of her."

"Your mom, is she still missing?"

"Yes."

"Any idea where she might be?"

Ruben shook his head.

"The police," Silas asked, "are they still looking for her?"

"Yeah, I guess."

"You should call and make sure the paperwork is current. When people aren't found right away, cops tend to stop looking. You know what they say: out of sight, out of mind."

"I can't do that."

"Why not?"

"Because I can't. Okay?"

"Easy. It was just a suggestion. I'll call them for you if you'd like."

"No, thanks. I think we'll leave it as it is."

When they reached the trash can, Silas lifted its lid and peered inside. He slapped Ruben on the back. "Will you look at that. Must be twenty or more cans in there. It's an honest-to-God treasure trove." He began pulling out aluminum cans and tossing them into the shopping cart.

After a time, he stopped, faced Ruben, and hooked a thumb toward the trash can. "You can get the rest."

Ruben edged forward so he could peer into the trash can. "You mean the gunky ones at the bottom?"

"Yeah. Them too."

What am I doing here? Ruben thought as he fished through the muck, the reality of his plight having become crystal clear. *Scrounging other people's garbage just for a few pennies. I can't go on living like this.* "That's the last of 'em." Ruben straightened up. "I need to wash my hands. I remember seeing a spigot back that way." Pushing the shopping cart, he headed off toward the south end of the park.

Silas followed but halted after twenty paces. He grabbed Ruben's arm and thrust his chin at an elderly lady seated on a nearby park bench. She seemed lost in thought.

Ruben regarded his companion with skepticism. "It's an old lady. What, you think she's going to mug us?" The woman had on a blue polka-dot dress and a moth-eaten overcoat that barely covered her knobby knees.

"Her purse. It's just sitting there on the bench beside her. She's not holding on to it or anything."

"And you want to steal it?"

Silas lowered his voice to a conspiratorial whisper. "Here's the plan. We'll split up. I'll circle around and come up on her from behind. You head over there about thirty yards in front of her. Make sure you're directly in her line of sight and start doing weird stuff but don't pay her any mind. Act like she's not even there. While she's checking you out, I'll grab her purse. You keep the cart with you, and we'll meet up by the entrance where we came in. We'll split fifty-fifty whatever she's got."

"Be serious. Look at her. She's probably as broke as we are."

"Anything is better than nothing."

"And then what is she gonna do? I wouldn't be surprised if all the money she has in the world is in that purse."

"All the better for us."

"Does she look like she can scrounge aluminum cans or panhandle? Hell, she's half-starved already. How is she going to fend for herself?"

"Why should we care? Her loss is our gain."

Ruben clenched his jaw. "I won't do it. It isn't right."

"Don't you go soft on me, not after I let you into my camp."

"How would you feel if someone took everything you had?"

"If I was foolish enough to leave my stuff out so they could steal it, that would be on me."

"You don't get it, do you? Some things are just wrong."

"Who are you to preach at me? Like you ain't never done nothing bad. What is it you're hiding anyway? What big secret are you protecting?"

"None of your damn business, and this has nothing to do with that. Just because I made a mistake once doesn't give me the right to make another one."

Silas threw up his hands in frustration. "Fine. If you won't help, I'll do it by myself. You just stand here and sing out if someone comes along."

"I'll do better than that. You go to steal her purse, and I'll start yelling at the top of my lungs."

Silas's eyes opened wide. "You're serious. After all I've done for you."

"Oh, that's right. You let me wallow in your miserable hovel. How kind."

"It's far better than the steam grate you were sleeping on."

"Look, forget the purse. Let's go sell these cans and use whatever money we get to buy breakfast. I'll treat."

Silas took a step back. "I don't think so. Seems to me this relationship is going nowhere. When we get back to camp, you gather up your stuff and take off. I'm done with you."

"If that's the way you feel, let's end it now. Why don't you take the cans, all of them, and we'll call it quits? You can also have whatever stuff I've left behind."

"You're kidding?"

"No, I'm not. Like you, I'm done but for different reasons. I'm not going to live like this any longer."

"What are you going to do?"

"The first thing I'm going to do is swallow my pride." Ruben thrust his hand into the pocket of his pants, confirming that the cell phone Reid had given him was still there. His fingers traced the reassuring smoothness of its glass face.

"What?"

"Never mind."

Silas's mood seemed to soften. "Look, Quick, maybe we're being a bit hasty—"

"No. You're right. It's time to make a change. I can't go on living hand to mouth. If I do, I'll slowly starve to death. Good luck to you. I wish you well. Truly, I do. And in case I haven't said it before, thanks for your hospitality." Reid turned and walked away, leaving the shopping cart behind.

Before heading for the exit, he detoured toward the park bench. After speaking with the old lady, he looked back at Silas and winked. He then strode off, shoulders back and head high.

The elderly lady grabbed her purse off the bench beside her and looped her arm securely through its straps.

The sun was sinking toward the horizon as Reid pulled into the parking lot at the Bright Star Motel. He had left work early after having met with Berlman Automotive's representative to discuss a few minor glitches.

With his guidance, things were progressing smoothly. Only a handful of last-minute tweaks would be needed to iron out the problems.

Beta testing on a fleet of rental cars was nearing completion, and the preliminary results were extremely favorable. By the end of the week, the final product would be ready for distribution to the major automotive manufacturers.

For this and other reasons, Reid was in very good spirits as he climbed the stairs to the upper level and knocked on the door to room 207.

"Who is it?" asked a male voice from inside the room.

"Who do you think?" Reid asked. "You expecting room service?" Since reconnecting with Quick, Reid had managed to stop by to check on his welfare every two to three days.

When the door opened, Quick stood facing him, shirtless and in his stocking feet. "You're early. I didn't expect you for another half hour."

"Our bug hunt wrapped up early, so I decided to beat the rush hour traffic. Are you hungry?"

"I'm always hungry. What's a bug hunt?"

"A line-by-line review of software code looking for errors." As Reid stepped into the room, he noted how his protégé had changed physically in three weeks since he had called asking for help. His eyes were clearer, he was putting on weight, and his face was less sallow.

More than that, his hair was combed, his nails were clean, and he smelled considerably better than when he had been sleeping on the streets. Bottom line, he no longer seemed the street denizen he had once been.

"What say we try that new chicken place," Reid suggested. "You know the one over on Rosewood."

"Whatever you think. Let me finish getting dressed."

Reid stepped into the kitchenette and opened the small fridge. "Looks like we need to stop by a supermarket on our way back. Your provisions are running low."

"Like I said, I'm hungry all the time." Quick fetched a lime-green sport shirt out of the closet. He slipped it on and began buttoning it up the front.

Reid's gaze scanned the apartment. Everything seemed shipshape. "You doing all right here?"

"I'm fine, thanks to you. By the way, Granger's Department Store called me in for a job interview this morning. I think they plan on hiring me. With luck, I can start Monday."

"That is excellent news. This truly is a red-letter day. Did they say what you'll be doing?" Reid sank down into the room's only armchair.

Seated on the end of the bed to put on his shoes, Quick said, "Starting out, I'll be a stock clerk in the warehouse. They implied that after I'm off probation and when a slot opens up on the floor, I can apply for a sales position."

"How do you feel about that?"

"I'm good with it." Quick seemed somewhat unsure.

"Don't BS me. How do you really feel?"

"A little worried, maybe. I ain't never done anything like this before."

"I *have never* done anything like this before," Reid corrected.

"You neither?" Quick retorted with feigned seriousness.

They both laughed.

It pleased Reid that the young man was in a cheerful frame of mind. He worried about the lingering psychological trauma his homelessness might have caused. "You know what this means, don't you?"

"What?"

"You're going to need better transportation than that pawnshop bicycle we've had you pedaling around on. I think tomorrow we should stop by the DMV and see about getting you a driver's license or at least a learner's permit. Then when you can drive legally, we can go shopping for a used car that will serve your needs—nothing fancy, but one that's in good condition."

The expression on Quick's face told that he could hardly believe his ears. "Are you serious?"

"Completely."

The young man's eyes became moist. "I don't know how, but I swear, one day, I will pay you back—every last penny."

"Let's get one thing straight. You don't owe me a dime. I'm doing this because I can and because I want to. Someday you'll meet someone in need, and when that happens, I'll expect you to pay it forward as they say. It's only proper that we pass on the blessings we receive."

Reid blinked as the words came out of his mouth. He tried to imagine the man he had once been saying such things. Who was this new guy? When had the transformation taken place? What he found amazing was that he had meant every word. "There is one thing you can do for me if you're willing." Reid uncrossed his legs and sat forward a little.

"Name it," Quick said with certitude.

"Don't you think it's time you told me your real name? Or do you still not trust me?"

Taken aback, Quick paled. He stood and faced away as if feeling threatened. At length, he turned back again and squared his shoulders. "My name is Reuben, Ruben Walker."

Reid stood and extended his hand. "Well then. How do you do, Ruben Walker? It's nice to meet you."

The young man hesitated but then returned the handshake.

"Now," Reid said, "I don't know about you, but I'm hungry. What say we grab some chow?"

"Sounds about right," Ruben spoke softly as if feeling vulnerable.

They left the motel together.

On the way to the restaurant, Ruben looked across from the passenger seat and said, "You've never actually told me. What is it you do exactly?"

"I'm a businessman. I run my own company. The software we create will let people experience the world around them more fully."

"Interesting."

"We think so."

Ruben stared out through the windshield at the road ahead. After a time, he said, "You're married, aren't you?"

"Yes. Allison and I have been together over twenty-one years now."

"And you have a son—"

"Had a son. He died."

"Sorry, man. That's sad. Truly. No other kids?"

"No."

"How old was he?"

"About your age, maybe a year older. His name was Connor. I miss him."

"I know what you mean. I miss my brothers and my sister."

"You've mentioned them before. I think you said you were trying to find them. Any luck?"

"None. I haven't seen or heard from them since they were taken away."

"I'm sure one day you'll be reunited."

"Yes, we will," Ruben declared with certainty.

As they neared the restaurant, Reid looked at his young passenger. "Tell me, Ruben, have you thought about your future and what you're going to do with your life?"

"Not really. I mean, right now it's like I'm living in a dream."

"Perhaps it's something we should talk about. The first thing you should do is get your GED."

"What's a GED?"

"General education diploma. It's equivalent to a high school diploma. With it you stand a much better chance of landing a good job, and you can go on to college if you choose."

"College? Me? Give me a break."

"Don't sell yourself short. You have the brains. All you lack is the education. Trust me. I employ computer programmers who aren't nearly as sharp as you are."

"Really?"

"Really, really."

They both laughed.

"One more thing," Reid added. "My wife and I would like to have you over for dinner on the Saturday after next. She's anxious to meet you. I think you and she will get along quite well. What do you say?"

"Sure. I mean, yes, thank you."

"Good." Reid parked the Lexus. "Now let's see if the chicken here is as good as they say."

❧❦❧

A little after 8:30 p.m. on a Saturday, Reid returned to the Silver Vale House after having dropped Ruben off at the Bright Star Motel.

Dinner had gone well. Allison and the young man had seemed to hit it off due in no small part to the wholesome meal she had prepared—pot roast with brown gravy, vegetables, and apple cobbler for dessert.

Not only had his protégé complimented Allison multiple times, but he had also asked for seconds and then thirds. When it came to eating, Ruben was a bottomless pit.

As Reid pulled into the garage, he noted Gavin Marsh's car parked out front. They had spoken at length the previous afternoon at work. Reid wracked his memory to recall whether there were any outstanding issues serious enough to warrant a late-night visit on a weekend. He could think of none.

After entering the house, Reid made his way to the kitchen. He found Gavin seated at the oval table in the breakfast nook, the last portions of a serving of pot roast and vegetables on the plate in front of him. Perhaps insatiable hunger was the explanation for his visit. The man had an incredible talent for sensing when a free meal was to be had.

Allison stood at the sink, washing dishes. Over her shoulder, she said to her husband as he entered the room, "I was just telling Gavin about Ruben and how you're helping him."

Gavin swallowed a mouthful of pot roast. "I hear you're looking to get him his own apartment and that you're even considering buying him a car?"

"Only after he gets his license." Reid filled a glass with ice water and sat down at the table. "Good pot roast, huh?" He took a sip.

"Oh yeah," Gavin chewed his final bite.

"So what's up?" Reid asked. "To what do we owe the honor of your presence?"

Gavin set his fork down on his plate and grinned. "I met someone."

"A woman, I presume," Reid said, "judging by your goofy affect."

"She is indeed. Her name is Rosemarie Brandeis, like the university. Everyone calls her Rosie. She's a secretary at Berlman Automotive. I met her about a week ago when she stopped by ERA to drop off some production estimates. We've dated three times now, including tonight."

Reid consulted his watch. "It must not have been much of a date for you to be done this early."

The color rose in Gavin's cheeks. "We're taking it slow."

Allison finished rinsing a dish and stacked it in the drainer. She then turned to face the table. "How wonderful for you, Gavin. Tell me about your new friend. How old is she? Is she single? Has she ever been married? She's not married now, is she?"

"She's in her midthirties I think. I haven't asked her age, but like me, she's never been married. And guess what? She collects Lalique crystal. Can you believe it? What are the odds? It's like we're made for each other."

"Well, congratulations!" Allison exclaimed brightly. "One day soon you'll have to bring her by so we can meet her."

"Indeed," Reid agreed. "I don't remember encountering anyone named Rosie who works for Berlman Automotive."

"You were out of the office when she stopped by," Gavin said.

"I see."

"If you're done with your meal—" Allison stepped forward to collect Gavin's plate. "Did you get enough?"

"Yes, thank you. It was delicious."

"Good." Allison thrust her chin in the direction of the den. "Now if you boys want to get out of here, I can finish cleaning up."

Reid stood. "As you wish." He gathered his wife into a hug and kissed her neck. "Thank you for fixing such a fine dinner. And thank you for helping put Ruben at ease."

"I did my best. I could tell he felt uncomfortable the way he kept looking around like he was in a foreign country."

"In one sense he was. Come on, Gavin. Let's get out of this lovely lady's hair."

The two men made their way to the den. As was their custom, Reid chose the overstuffed armchair, Gavin the couch.

As he sat down, Reid caught a glimpse of Connor's drawing. The flying sparrow drawn with pastel pencils on sanded paper hung in a silver frame in a place of honor. A lump caught in Reid's throat as he again lamented the loss of such obvious talent. Other memories followed, and he struggled to keep his thoughts from hurtling down familiar tracks that led to anger and despair.

"Are you sure you know what you're doing?" Gavin asked as they settled in.

"What? Oh, you mean with Ruben?"

Gavin nodded.

"I think so. Why? What's your concern?"

"You seem to be investing a lot of time and money into someone you've only recently met. How do you know you can trust this kid? People are forced to live on the streets for a reason.

"Usually it's because they can no longer cope with a normal lifestyle. Either they're burned out on drugs or they have PTSD or some other psychological injury that makes them incapable of functioning normally.

"Most of them are addicts, and most of the addicts are thieves or worse. I'm just concerned you might be putting yourself in harm's way."

Reid gave a dismissive wave with his hand. "Ruben isn't like that. He's a good kid who's had some tough breaks."

"How do you know?"

"Because I hired a private investigator to check him out. He's the oldest of four siblings. His mother was doing her best to raise her children, but then one day, she simply disappeared. The police investigated, but there was no trace of where she might have gone. Then the authorities gave up looking.

"Child Protective Services took the kids and put them in foster homes, but Ruben kept running away. That's how he wound up living on the street.

"The one thing he wants most in the world is to see his family reunited. If I can help by getting him to the point where he can pay rent and put food on the table, maybe he can see his wish fulfilled."

"And you're doing this out of the kindness of your heart?"

"Second Corinthians chapter 9 verse 6 says, 'Whoever sows sparingly will reap sparingly. Whoever sows generously will reap generously.' And somewhere else, the Bible says, 'Never grow weary of doing good.' As Christians, isn't that what we're supposed to do—help others?"

"You consider yourself a Christian now," Gavin said in amazement.

"I do, and it's your fault," Reid replied. "You're the one who told me to talk to Jesus, and I did. I asked Him to come into my life and help me. And now I can't explain it, but somehow I feel different inside."

"Different how?"

"It's hard to put into words—less stressed—more aware of the plight of the people I meet."

"Are these feelings the reason you've taken this kid on as your own personal rescue project?"

"Partially, I suspect. But it's more than that.

"There's something about Ruben I can relate to. In many ways, he reminds me of Connor. When we're together, he fills the space around us with echoes of my son. In a way, it's like I've been given a second chance at being a dad."

"What about your search for Connor's killer? How do you stand with your quest for revenge?"

"Those feelings are still there," Reid admitted bitterly.

"So how do you reconcile your desire for revenge with being a follower of Jesus?"

"That's a damn good question, and I don't have an answer."

"Does that mean you're not ready to forgive?"

"Forgive? Never. When they strap Connor's killer into the electric chair, I'll throw the switch myself."

10

REVELATION

Early February 2018

Eight months after first meeting Ruben, Reid stood on the balcony of the young man's studio apartment. Ruben was still in the bathroom, getting himself ready to leave.

The view beyond the balcony left a lot to be desired, but the rent was cheap. Most importantly, the residential complex was located only a quarter mile from Granger's Department Store, where Ruben was currently employed.

On the streets below, people were coming and going, though foot traffic seemed about average for a Sunday morning.

Reid reflected upon his young protégé and how their relationship had strengthened, especially in recent months. Gone was the initial distrust that had been so evident. In its place, a bond of genuine friendship, bolstered by kindness and mutual respect, had emerged.

Reid clasped his hands behind his back as he considered the one thing that still troubled him. Like a splinter in a festering wound or a nagging toothache, some deep hurt was causing Ruben considerable anguish. Every effort to bring the issue to light and discuss it openly had been rebuffed. Whatever secret the young man was guarding had to be formidable indeed.

After stepping back inside the apartment, Reid pulled the sliding glass door shut. Through the partially ajar bathroom door, he caught a glimpse of Ruben's reflection in the mirror. "Aren't you ready yet? You've been preening for twenty minutes."

"Almost," Ruben called out as he applied a few final touchups with his comb. Eventually, he emerged with a flourish. "Gotta look good for the ladies in church."

"We're not going to church."

"Then why am I wearing my Sunday finest?"

"Because I have a surprise for you."

"You and your surprises. Where are we headed this time?"

"You'll see."

"Will Allison be joining us?"

"She very much wants to, but the choir director convinced her that the soprano section would sound miserably thin without her."

Ruben's brow furrowed with a look of speculative contemplation. "So Allison doesn't need to be there. Anything we need to take with us?"

"Such as—"

"Oh, I don't know. It's your surprise."

"Quit fishing and let's go. If we don't get a move on, we'll be late."

"So your surprise is time-sensitive—an event then—perhaps a movie, a performance? I know—a party."

"Give it a rest. By the way, how are your studies coming along?" Reid indicated the collection of textbooks lying open on the narrow coffee table.

"Math and science are good. English is okay. History and social studies bore me to tears."

"Will you be ready to test next month?"

"I should be."

"I assume you know how important getting your GED is."

"Not really. I guess I wasn't paying attention the last hundred times you told me. Say, will I need my jacket?"

"Probably not."

"So this event will be indoors. Hey, I've got it—the grand opening of a new computer store?"

"Do you want a hint?"

"Nah, it's more fun floundering around like a complete idiot. Of course I want a hint."

"We're going to a mall," Reid said with a sly smile.

"You call that a hint?"

"Would you rather stand here and play twenty questions or find out firsthand?"

Without further urging, Ruben headed for the door. "If you're waiting on me, you're wasting time." As he led the way down the stairs to the first level, he looked back and said, "Is there some big shindig going on I should know about?"

"Not that I'm aware of. Look, you're never going to guess it. You might as well relax and enjoy the journey."

"Guessing is half the fun."

Reid grinned. "Oh, I doubt that very much, as I'm sure you'll agree when you see what's in store for you. For now, though, you're just going to have to wait."

The Three Winds Mall was bustling with activity when Ruben and Reid arrived.

Two years earlier, a consortium of retailers had joined forces to build the mall in Palo Alto's northern suburbs. The three-story shopping multiplex, with its various entertainment venues, had rapidly become a popular hangout, especially on weekends. Crowds of shoppers, mostly teenagers, thronged the main concourse.

Ruben eyed the hordes with a sense of wonder, this being his first visit. The noise and tumult he found a bit daunting. Twelve months earlier, any notion of loitering in a place where he couldn't afford even the cheapest curios would have seemed absurd. As he listened to snippets of conversation, he had the odd impression that the teenagers near his own age were speaking a foreign language.

Twenty yards inside the main entrance, Ruben paused to scan the mall's spacious interior. His gaze drifted from storefront to storefront and from kiosk to advertising display to the main informational bulletin boards.

Taking it all in at once proved impossible. There was simply too much information to process. With care, he went back and studied his surroundings a second time, seeking evidence of a special event or some unique happening.

"Impressive, is it not?" Reid asked, having halted beside him.

"I never would have believed there was this much stuff for sale in the whole world."

Reid's brow furrowed in a scowl. "My friend, what you're witnessing is the plague of modern society: rampant consumerism. Slick advertising creates a demand for products that people neither need nor can afford.

"We're made to feel incomplete if we can't lay our hands upon the latest, the best, or the most highly sought-after gadget, toy, or whatever. Shopping has become the universal antidote for loneliness. It's the primary refuge for people who live unfulfilled lives."

"Wow. Sounds like you're not a fan." Ruben cast a sidelong glance at his mentor.

"I used to be. In fact, I was as gullible as the next guy. But not that long ago, my priorities changed. These days, I measure my self-worth by something other than what I own."

"So why'd you bring me here?"

"To meet someone." Reid turned and headed toward the central elevators. "This way."

"Where are we going?"

"To the food court."

Ruben grinned. "I like the sound of that."

The ride to the second floor passed quickly. When the doors swooshed open, Reid and Ruben stepped out of the elevator.

The first thing Ruben noticed was a relative absence of commotion. Apparently, it was still too early for hunger to fill the food court with noisy throngs.

Looking around, he noticed nothing unusual. No one seemed particularly keyed up. Nothing interesting was going on. Feeling confused, he began studying the faces of the people seated at various tables.

An instant later, his gaze settled on a face that seemed evocatively familiar. He squinted as his brain strained to identify features that were well-known yet somehow changed. The flash of recognition came with a start.

"Travis!" Ruben shrieked. Twenty-two months had elapsed since he had last laid eyes on his brother's face, but there was no denying the kid seated halfway across the food court was his younger sibling.

Reid hastily grabbed the back of Ruben's shirt to keep him from rushing off. "Hang on a sec, sport. There are a few ground rules you'll need to keep in mind. Your brother's foster parents have agreed to this meeting with a couple stipulations.

"First, do nothing to undermine their authority. Travis is a member of their family now, and you will honor that relationship.

"Also, his parents insist on supervising any future meetings you might have with your brother. That means you two can't arrange something on your own. Remember, Travis is still a minor, and they have full legal custody. You must never attempt to contact him without their knowledge. Do you agree to these conditions?"

"Yes," Ruben blurted out as he strove to break free.

Reid kept a tight grip. "Look me in the eye and give me your word. It was hard enough convincing them to agree to this visit. I need your promise that you will do nothing to split their family apart. Do you promise?"

Ruben ceased his struggles. "Why would you think I would do that?"

"Because I know how desperately you want to put your family back together. But this isn't the time, nor is it the place. This is a social visit, pure and simple—a chance for the two of you to catch up, and that's all. Now promise me."

"I promise."

"Good." Reid released his grip.

Instead of darting off, Ruben peered into his benefactor's face. "How did you find him?"

"I talked to Ms. Bartholomew, your caseworker. That's right. Child Protective Services still has an open file on you. She got in touch with Travis's foster parents and opened negotiations to set up this visit."

"You've been in contact with my caseworker!" Ruben exclaimed with incredulity.

"I had to. Legally you're still a ward of the court. I've been keeping her updated as to your progress, but don't worry. For now, she's more than happy to let things stand as they are."

"What did she say about me?"

"Nothing bad, I assure you. Why?"

"Never mind." A split second later, Ruben was scurrying between tables toward his brother.

Ruben and Travis sat down opposite one another at an isolated table, some distance away from other people.

During the introductions, Ruben had covertly checked out Travis's foster parents. Being middle-aged and unremarkably ordinary in appearance, the couple had seemed exactly the sort to invite wayward children into their home. Although a bit reserved, they had conversed pleasantly enough. Still, he had elected to withhold judgment as to whether or not he liked them. He would wait until he had gotten to know them better.

"Have you heard from Mom?" Travis asked in a soft tone of voice as they sat down.

"No. You heard anything?"

"Nothing." Travis's brow furrowed. "What do you suppose happened to her?"

"I have no idea. I keep imagining different explanations. It's a mystery why she disappeared like she did. It doesn't make any sense. Something bad must have happened."

"Do you think she'll come back?"

Ruben regarded his brother with a level gaze. "Never give up hope. If Mom can, she will. I know that for a fact. I feel it here." He tapped the center of his chest. "What about the twins? Have you heard from them?"

Travis shook his head.

"Me neither. Maybe Reid can track them down like he did you."

Travis looked to where the adults were seated. "He's not your foster parent, is he?"

"No. Just a friend."

"How did you guys meet?"

Ruben gave an abbreviated account of how, after running away from his fourth foster home, he had wound up living on the streets. He told about visiting the Bedrock Rescue Mission and how Reid had found him shivering on the sidewalk with pneumonia. He then sketched out a bare-bones history of how his life had turned around during the subsequent months. He intentionally avoided any mention of the robbery and the murder he had committed, though they were foremost in his thoughts.

Finishing up, Ruben said, "Reid owns a software development company. His program has something to do with how people experience the world around them. He's promised that after I get my diploma, I can come work for him if I want, or I can continue my education. Either way, he'll help."

"Man, you got lucky," Travis said when his older brother fell silent.

"Tell me about it. What about you? Look at how you've grown. What's your life like these days?"

"It's good. The Drakes, Ellen and Russell, are okay people. There's another foster kid who lives with us. His name is William. He's seven. He's gone through some bad times too. It's like living with the twins again. I get to be the big brother. I kind of like it."

"Do they treat you well?"

"I guess. Sometimes it gets boring, but they do the best they can. So you were living on the street? What was that like?"

"It was hard. Lonely mostly. I missed you guys so much. Nights were the worst. You have to worry about getting beat up and having your stuff stolen, and it's mostly at night when you realize you're all alone. Nobody cares if you live or die."

"I'm glad you didn't die."

"Yeah, me too. Something I learned: When you're on your own, it's easy to get into trouble." Ruben eyed his younger brother, who appeared to be wrestling with his own memories. "You know what I'm talking about. Something happened to you, didn't it? What was it? Did you get into trouble?"

"Once. I did something stupid. I knew it was wrong, but I was mad because our family had been split up. Ellen had this necklace. It had a long gold chain and a big stone with lots of colors in the middle. I took it and passed it on to the older brother of a kid in my class. He pawned it and gave me half the money.

"For a time, I figured I'd gotten away with being a thief, but then I kept remembering what Mom used to tell us about how we need to take responsibility for the things we do. So I admitted what I'd done.

"At first, I thought they were going to send me away. But they forgave me and let me do home chores to earn money so I could pay Ellen back. It's not a lot of fun feeling guilty inside."

Ruben winced as if a great weight had been laid on his soul. "No. It is not." He abruptly changed the subject. "When they split us up, I promised myself that one day I'd get us back together. I know I swore I wouldn't do anything to hurt your relationship with the Drakes, but do you think one day we might be a family again, assuming we can find the twins?"

"Maybe." Travis pondered the matter for a time. "Actually I guess I'm okay with where I am for now. Maybe we should leave things as they are."

Ruben's dejection strengthened. "If that's what you want—"

The siblings talked a while longer until the adults signaled it was time to go.

As Ruben accompanied Reid down the elevator and out of the mall, his heart was deeply troubled. His conversation with his younger brother had stirred up terrible memories and awakened vexing emotions he had done his best to put to rest.

Meeting with his younger sibling had not been the joyous reunion he had envisioned.

Reid sat at the oval table in the kitchen of the Silver Vale House. Ruben sat opposite him.

After leaving the Three Winds Mall, Reid had invited his young friend home for Sunday dinner. Reid and Allison had already discussed the matter and had agreed that a Sunday feast would make an appropriate setting for the next surprise they had planned.

Standing at the stove, Allison switched on the light in the oven to check on the casserole. Satisfied that the dish was cooking as it should, she straightened up. "I'm so glad you agreed to join us," she said to Ruben as she stirred a boiling pot of green beans. Tuna casserole, green beans, French bread, and apple pie à la mode were on the menu.

"I appreciate the invite," Ruben replied.

Allison smoothed her apron at her waist. "Ruben, are you okay? You seem troubled. Did your visit with your brother not go well?"

"No, it was great. I'm glad he's in a good place with a family who will look after him."

"But you still want him to live with you," Reid commented.

"Of course I do—the twins as well." Ruben glanced across the table. "Do you think I could visit with them like I did with Travis?"

Reid pursed his lips. "I asked. Their foster parents said no—for the time being at least. They think it would be too traumatic. Seeing you would remind them of having lost their mother. Perhaps when they're older—"

"Our mother is not lost. She's just not here right now."

"You know what I mean. The twins are younger than you and Travis. It's been especially hard on them having their family split up as it was. Only now are they adapting to their new environment."

Standing in front of the stove, Allison cleared her throat. "Dinner will take at least another half hour. If you boys would like to go for a walk or something, you have time." She gave her husband a knowing look.

Jokingly Reid suggested, "Sounds like the cook is telling us to get lost. Come on, sport. Grab your jacket. Let's stretch our legs."

"Where are we headed?" Ruben asked as the two men exited the front door together.

"To the park. It's only a few blocks from here."

For a time, they walked in silence. Then the distant rumble of an aircraft's engines caused Ruben to look up. High overhead, the plane's snowy contrail bisected the late afternoon sky.

"I wonder where they're headed," he mused.

Reid looked up as well. "Somewhere exotic probably. Have you ever thought about traveling?"

"Seriously? I'd still be stuck in East Palo Alto if it wasn't for you."

Reid gave a nod of acknowledgment as they continued on their way.

As they neared the park, he said, "There's something I've been meaning to tell you. I think you know how fond we are of you, but more than that, one of our greatest joys has been watching you turn your life around. Truly, it's been like receiving a gift we didn't deserve."

"How can you say that? How can you consider it a gift when I'm the one who's been gifted by your generosity? If not for you, I'd most likely be dead."

Reid halted at the edge of the park. He turned to face Ruben. "When you have children of your own, I think you'll understand." He then turned and continued walking.

With astonishment, Ruben said as he hurried to catch up, "Children? Aren't we rushing things a bit? Before I have children, I'll need a wife. And before I get a wife, I'll need a better job. And before I get a better job, I'll need a car. And somewhere along the line, I'll have to get myself an education."

"All in good time."

The two men tracked the asphalt path that circled the periphery of the park. As they approached the eastern boundary, Reid declared, "There's something else I've been meaning to tell you. It's a feeling Allison and I have shared for months now, but recently it's grown much stronger. Ruben, you may have already guessed this, but we've come to regard you as our son."

"I know what you mean. I have the same feelings. There are times when I think of you as the dad I never had, and Allison is my second mom."

"I am so glad you feel that way because Allison and I have talked it over, and we're in agreement. With your consent, we would like to adopt you. We would like you to become a true member of our family—if you'll have us."

Ruben's face twisted up with a look of dismay. "That's not a good idea. There are things about me you don't know—things I've never told you, bad things."

"I can't imagine there's much you could say that would change our minds. Look, you don't have to decide this very instant. Take your time. Give it some thought. You have a birthday coming up in April. You'll be eighteen. Give yourself until then to decide how you feel."

"Sure," Ruben replied as if deeply conflicted.

A gust of wind ruffled the carpet of eucalyptus leaves beside the path. "You know," Reid said in a soft voice, "it was over there where Connor died." He pointed to a spot ten yards away. "That was the exact spot."

"What!" Ruben exclaimed in horror.

"One shot to the forehead. We still don't know who did it."

Ruben took a step backward and looked around in panic. "Wait. I know this place. Oh my god. This is where it happened. This is—" Shaking his head, he backed away another step. "No. No. No. We shouldn't be here. This is wrong." He began trembling so badly he nearly stumbled. "Oh god, I can't—I'm sorry. Please, no."

"Ruben, what's the matter?"

Fighting back the tears that had welled up in his eyes, Ruben cried out, "You never told me your son was murdered."

"Yes, I did."

"No, you didn't! Never. All you've ever said was he died. I would have remembered. Oh god. This can't be. Why did you bring me here?"

"What's going on?"

"It was me," Ruben blurted out as if his secret and finally become too heavy to bear any longer. "I was the one. I shot him. It was an accident, I swear. All I meant to do was rob him. He lunged at me. The gun went off. I couldn't—there wasn't—it happened so fast."

"What?" Reid struggled to make sense of what he was hearing. "I don't understand. Are you saying it was you? You're the one who killed my son?"

"It was an accident."

"An accident? You murdered my son!"

"I didn't mean to. It just happened. I give you my word."

"Your word? The word of a murderer?" Reid's hands balled into fists. He hunched his shoulders and stepped forward. "All this time—all I've done for you, and now you tell me this?"

"I didn't know, man. I didn't know the guy I killed was your son. I swear."

"You must have known. How could you not? His picture is hanging in our home."

"The man I shot; I never saw his face. It was dark, and it happened too fast. Yes, I've seen your son's picture, but I didn't recognize him."

A blinding rage gripped Reid. He drew his fist back to launch a furious attack but then froze.

A twisted tangle of conflicting emotions had locked his arm in a cocked position. He struggled mightily to let his fury to have its way, but he could not deliver the punch. Gradually he lowered his fist.

"What are we going to do?" Ruben asked, his eyes wide with fear and his face pallid in the evening light.

With icy calmness, Reid replied, "I'm going to take you back to your apartment."

"And then?"

"That's yet to be decided."

Gavin Marsh answered his front door wearing a terry cloth bathrobe over his plaid pajamas. "What time is it?" he mumbled, stifling a yawn.

Reid stood facing him. His clothes were rumpled, and his hair was tousled. Dark circles shadowed his eyes, and the lines etched into his face gave testimony to the agony he felt inside. "Sometime after 2:00 a.m., I think. I'm not sure."

Gavin blinked to clear his vision. "You look terrible. What's going on?"

"I need to talk to you. May I come in?"

Gavin seemed to be on the verge of saying something like "Can't this wait?" but then changed his mind. "Sure. You're always welcome. I'll put some coffee on. I assume this has something to do with why you weren't at work yesterday?" Gavin plodded sleepily toward the back of the house.

As Reid followed, he said, "It does. For two nights now, I haven't been able to sleep. I'm literally torn up inside. I don't know what I'm supposed to do. Hell, I'm not even sure how I'm supposed to feel. I was hoping you could help me sort things out."

"I'll try."

The two men stood facing one another in the kitchen. Gavin said, "Why don't you start at the beginning?"

Fighting to restrain his seething emotions, Reid laid out the horrible secret that Ruben had revealed. Twice, he nearly lost his composure.

For a time, Gavin stood immobile. Then his eyes narrowed. "You're telling me Ruben Walker is the guy who shot Connor?"

"I heard it straight from his own lips. He knew details that never made it into the press."

"I find this hard to accept. Are you sure he's not pulling your leg? No, that would be beyond the pale. He seemed like such a nice kid."

Reid grimaced. "Yes, he did, and that's my problem."

"When he told you, what did you do?" Gavin asked.

"Nothing."

"Nothing? You didn't go to the police?"

"I decided to wait."

"Does Allison know any of this?"

"I haven't had the heart to tell her. She cares as much for Ruben as I did. When I tell her, it will be like losing our son all over again."

"I can imagine. How can I help?"

"I need to figure out what I'm supposed to do. I was hoping maybe you could help me put things in perspective."

Gavin tensed. As if on the verge of giving advice, he hesitated and then instead said, "What does your heart tell you to do?"

"One minute I want to reap my vengeance upon him—to see him dead. The next I want to protect him from the agony I know he's feeling. Deep inside he's a good kid. I get that—a good kid who did a terrible thing. Can you believe it? What are the odds that my son's killer is the one person I would choose to befriend?"

"It does seem highly coincidental." Gavin cocked his head slightly. "Do you think God's hand might have been in the way things are working out?"

"That possibility has occurred to me."

"And—"

Reid shrugged. "I can't decide what I'm supposed to do or what I'm supposed to learn or how I'm supposed to feel. Everything is jumbled up. One minute I'm furious. The next minute I want to bawl my eyes out. Like I said, I haven't been able to sleep for all the turmoil. I feel like what Adam must have felt after Cain slew Abel."

Gavin's mood became even more somber. "I think I'm sensing what's really troubling you. In the past, we've talked about forgiveness. Well, this is where it gets real."

"Forgiveness. Right. Forgive to be forgiven. How?"

Gavin braced his backside against the kitchen counter. "When you accepted Jesus into your life, God forgave you for your sins, did He not?"

Reid nodded. "He did."

"So how did God forgive you?"

"What do you mean?"

"How was it that God, who is absolutely holy and righteous, was able to forgive you—you being a sinner and undeniably worthy of judgment?"

"Jesus's sacrifice on the cross paid for my sins."

"Right, Jesus died for you. So what are sins? Aren't they, in fact, disobedience born of the choices we make?"

"I guess so. Yes."

"So in essence what you're saying is that you killed God's son. It was your sins, the choices you made, that were directly responsible for His death. Yet God was able to forgive you."

A heavy silence filled the room.

A minute later, Reid glanced up from having been staring at nothing. "Forgive to be forgiven—forgiven to forgive. I think I get it." He straightened up.

Gavin tilted his head with an inquisitive look. "What are you going to do?"

"I haven't decided, but I sense that God might be working within me. Perhaps I should just trust Him."

❧❦❧

Standing on the sidewalk in front of the Atherton Arms residential complex, Reid stared up at the small balcony that fronted Ruben's studio apartment. The hour was late, and a light was on behind the drawn curtains.

Five days had passed since he had called upon Gavin in the wee hours of the morning. For as long as he could, he had put off what he was about to do, but the time had finally come to deal with the conflicts that raged within him. Even so, given the slightest excuse, he would have turned and fled.

Steeling himself, Reid climbed the stairs to the main corridor on the second floor. When he knocked on Ruben's door, there was no response. He knocked again and then a third time.

After a long interval and having received no reply, he used his spare key to unlock the door. Through a tiny crack, he called out, "Ruben, are you in there? It's me, Reid. We need to talk."

Silence.

Reid pushed the door open wider and peered inside. Soda cans, empty pizza cartons, and other refuse lay scattered across the floor. The bed was rumpled, the sheets and blankets lying half on and half off the mattress. In the middle of the bed lay a body.

For a moment, Reid feared that he was looking at another tragedy, but then a voice came from the middle of the bed. "Are you alone?"

"I am," Reid said.

"You didn't bring the police?"

"Nope. It's just me. All right if I come in?" Cautiously Reid stepped inside the studio apartment and closed the door behind him. Glancing around, he took note of the scattered debris. "Seems like the housekeepers haven't been doing their job." His attempt at levity fell miserably flat. "How are you?"

"What do you want?" Stirring for the first time, Ruben sat up on the edge of the bed. He looked as though he too had been plagued by sleepless nights.

"I want to talk. We have things to work out between us."

"I'm surprised you haven't turned me in."

"And I'm surprised you're still here. You've had opportunity enough to get away."

"I couldn't face the thought of hiding again." Ruben stood and headed toward the bathroom. Reid could hear water running.

When Ruben emerged, he was drying his hands and face. He cast the hand towel onto the bed. Standing five feet apart, the two men eyed each other warily.

"You know," Ruben said, "I was hoping you might show up."

"Were you? Why?"

"Because I wanted to tell you how sorry I am. What I did was probably the worst thing anyone can imagine. To take a human life— there is no excuse that makes it okay. Every day I've wished I could undo the harm I've caused, make it so it never happened. But I can't. Believe me. If I could trade places with Connor, I would—in a heartbeat.

"Reid, you're a good and decent man, and Allison is a good and decent woman. You two don't deserve the pain I've caused you. All I can say is I'm sorry. I know it doesn't count for much, but I mean it with all my heart."

"Thank you for that."

"So what are you going to do now that you know the truth?"

Reid squared his shoulders. "I'm going to forgive you. That doesn't mean I can forget what happened. It doesn't mean I'm okay with losing my son. I'm not. What it does mean is that I no longer feel compelled to take my revenge upon you. As far as I'm concerned, your debt to me has been set aside."

Ruben had been holding himself stiffly. The tension seemed to bleed out of his muscles. His relief was evident on his face. "I can't tell you how much this means to me. I know I don't deserve it."

"None of us deserves the forgiveness we receive. You know there's another question that demands an answer," Reid said solemnly.

"Which is—"

"What are *you* going to do now?"

"Meaning?"

"Do you intend to turn yourself in, or will you continue to guard your secret?"

"Turn myself in? I thought you just forgave me?"

"I did forgive you. As far as I'm concerned, this matter has been put to rest. My son is dead. Nothing will bring him back. But I'm not the only one you must answer to. You need to choose wisely where you go from here. The quality of your future life—indeed the serenity of your soul— will depend upon what decision you make. Your guilt will continue to haunt you until you make yourself accountable for what you've done."

"If I turn myself in, what will the authorities do?"

"That's hard to say for sure. You committed murder while attempting a robbery. That's a class A felony. But there are mitigating factors: You were a juvenile at the time of the crime. You were in extreme distress because of your homelessness, your separation from your family, and being half starved to death.

"Since the crime, you've conducted yourself as a model citizen. You've gotten a job. You're supporting yourself. You're working on your education. And you haven't gotten into any more trouble. Besides, turning yourself in will count for a great deal.

"You should know that Allison and I intend to stand as character witnesses at your trial. If you throw yourself on the mercy of the court, I'm inclined to believe the judge will be lenient when it comes to your sentencing. What's more, we'll help defend you with the best legal representation available."

"You two would do that for me in spite of what I did?"

"We would."

"Why?"

"Because, as we've said before, we love you and because we've prayed about it, and God told us it is the right thing to do."

Seven months after visiting Ruben's apartment to offer forgiveness, Reid sat beside Allison in a small conference room just off the judge's chambers. They were alone. Judge Roy Grim, senior justice of the Superior Court of San Mateo, had allowed them use of the space prior to the sentencing hearing that was soon to begin.

"How do you think his sentencing will go?" Allison asked.

"Well enough," Reid replied, "assuming the judge approves the plea agreement. He can set it aside if he chooses, but I doubt that he will, not with the prosecutor's strong recommendation."

"Oh, I do hope you're right." Allison seemed troubled, but Reid could tell there was more on her mind than just the sentencing hearing.

Taking hold of his wife's hand, Reid felt a shiver pass through her body. He said, "Are you sure you want to go through with this?"

"I am," Allison declared with confidence.

"You don't have any doubts? If you do, now is the time to say so."

Allison inhaled deeply and then let out a slow breath. "Losing a child is the worst tragedy a mom can endure. It's like part of you is torn away, leaving you less than you were.

"Yet unlike you, I was more wounded than angry. Now those feelings are mostly gone. When I think about Ruben and how close we've become—in his heart, he's a good kid.

"Of that I'm certain. He never meant to do what he did, and I believe he's suffered as much as we have. So yes, I'm sure. What about you? How do you feel?"

Reid closed his eyes to gaze inside himself. "I remember our conversations—all the times we've talked this over." He opened his eyes to look directly at his wife. "I believed I was being truthful when I told you I wanted to proceed, but then I'd find myself wondering, 'Are we doing the right thing?' I keep asking myself, 'How do I really feel? What is my heart telling me to do?'

"Like you, I believe Ruben is fundamentally a good person who made some terrible choices, and I have no doubt that I have forgiven him.

"But this decision we're making, it cuts deeper than that. In a way, it's more about who we are, or more accurately it's about who we wish to become. Can we truly learn to love unconditionally without harboring any lingering malice?

"I stopped by the cemetery yesterday to visit Connor's grave and ask his advice. Looking down at his headstone, I laid out what we were contemplating. As I recounted the things we've discussed, a sense of peace came over me—a feeling of serenity as deep as any I've known. I'm certain he approves. So yes. Like you, I'm sure."

Allison gave her husband's hand a loving squeeze.

The side door opened. Two sheriff's deputies escorted Ruben into the room. Their badges reflected the glow of the fluorescent lights overhead.

Ruben's eyes looked haggard, but his hair was combed, and he was clean-shaven. He broached a feeble smile. "How do you like the suit? Pretty fancy, huh? My lawyer insisted that I wear it. I had to have help with the tie."

Ruben went to raise his hands to his throat, but the handcuffs that circled his wrists were bound to a chain around his waist. When he took a step forward, the shackles on his ankles rattled.

The two deputies migrated to opposite corners of the cramped room. Their attention remained focused on their prisoner. Reid did his best to ignore them.

"Are you nervous?" Allison asked, but she then flushed with embarrassment. "Of course you are. So are we. What did your lawyer say? Has he heard anything new? Has anything changed?"

"He doesn't foresee a problem." Ruben seemed resigned to whatever fate awaited him as he sat down facing his visitors. "As far as I know, the sentence will be twelve to twenty-five years with a possibility of parole in six."

"And you're okay with that?" Reid asked.

"In truth, I'm terrified, but it's far better than what I expected."

"You should know," Reid admitted, "that it's been difficult for us these past months, not knowing what the final ruling will be."

"Yes, it has," Allison agreed. "But no matter what happens going forward, we intend to be there for you. We plan on visiting you every week."

Reid nodded. "That's right. We will support you every way we can. We'll help with your education while you're inside, and when you get out, you'll have a job waiting for you at ERA if you want it.

"Look, we don't have much time, and there are a couple things we need to tell you. First off, we want you to know how proud we are. It took true courage to take responsibility for what you did. I know the judge was impressed."

"Yes, he was," Allison added. "You could see it in the way he looked at you when you pleaded guilty."

"That's right." Reid gave a nod of affirmation. "We also know what this has meant to you—forsaking your goal of seeing your siblings reunited. I suspect surrendering your dream was the most difficult part of your decision."

Choked up with emotion, Ruben seemed unable to respond.

Reid glanced at his wife and smiled as he squeezed her hand. He then looked directly at Ruben. "Do you remember what we talked about in the park about adopting you as our son? Well, that offer still stands—if you're willing.

"We've spoken with Judge Grim. The preliminary paperwork has been submitted. He's prepared to go forward with the ceremony today if you're in agreement. What do you say? Will you become a member of our family?"

A solitary tear trailed down Ruben's cheek. "I can't believe you still want me."

"We love you, Ruben," Reid declared with profound sincerity.

"But I—"

"Yes, you did. But God loves us despite our faults and unrighteous behaviors. Can we do any less? We are who we are, each of us, a tangled mess of good and evil.

"In this world, awful things happen. We do the best we can, but sometimes things go horribly wrong. When they do, the only virtue that makes life worthwhile is love. What do you say? Will you be our son?"

The side door opened, and the bailiff stepped into the room. "The judge is on his way to the courtroom. It's time to get these proceedings started."

Ruben stood up. As soon as he moved, the two deputies stepped forward, each taking hold of an arm.

A joyous smile spread across Ruben's face as he looked down at his visitors. "I love you guys, both of you. You are the kindest, most caring people I know. So yes. Yes. Oh yes. I would be honored to become your son."

The End